She had lashed Aton's wrists while he was barely conscious, leaving him pinned on his back, his arms stretched out on either side. The brown stems anchoring him were about four inches thick at the base, and seemed deeply rooted. there was no way to pull free.

"I'll be watching you for the next couple of days," she said. "With any luck, it'll take that long."

He felt sharp, stabbing pain as a leechworm fastened itself to his flesh, and he realized that the torture was starting already. He mashed the creature into the ground, closed his eyes, and shuddered.

When he opened his eyes again, she was bending over him. "Your pain gives me more pleasure than you ever did while you were alive."

She turned away from him and walked back to the ship, pausing when she reached the hatch. "One thing you should know. There are more than a thousand parasites and predators on this planet. Most of them come out at night. I think it should be dark in an hour or so. . . ."

SOMA

Piers Anthony's Worlds of Chthon

Charles Platt

A SIGNET BOOK

NEW AMERICAN LIBRARY

Copyright © 1988 by Piers Anthony Jacob and Charles Platt

 SIGNET TRADEMARK REG. U.S. PAT. OFF. AND FOREIGN COUNTRIES
REGISTERED TRADEMARK—MARCA REGISTRADA
HECHO EN CHICAGO, U.S.A.

SIGNET, SIGNET CLASSIC, MENTOR, ONYX, PLUME, MERIDIAN
and NAL BOOKS are published by NAL PENGUIN INC.,
1633 Broadway, New York, New York 10019

First Printing, January, 1989

1   2   3   4   5   6   7   8   9

PRINTED IN THE UNITED STATES OF AMERICA

Author's Note

This is the fourth book set in the Chthon universe. Preceding titles are *Chthon*, *Phthor*, and *Plasm*, the first two being by Piers Anthony, the third by Charles Platt. *Soma* begins approximately six months after events at the conclusion of *Plasm*.

Several characters and environments recur in all four novels. At the same time, however, *Soma* tells a self-contained story that can be read and enjoyed on its own.

The reader is asked to remember that this is a science-fiction adventure whose characters should not be seen as role models for people in the real world.

SOMA

1.

The rocky floor of the passageway trembled beneath his feet. Aton steadied himself against a nearby boulder and peered into semidarkness. He held his breath and listened. He heard no sound in the vast network of caverns, yet he knew the caterpillar was out there.

He turned to his companion. Her red hair gleamed dully in the eerie luminescence shed by patches of lichen on the roof of the passageway. Her young body was loosely clad in a ragged convict's tunic. Her face, serenely beautiful, was turned toward him. "Malice," he said softly. He reached out and touched her cheek.

The ground shook once more, and this time a distant eerie shriek echoed through the maze of caves and lava tubes. Aton felt a chill across his shoulders, though the air in the cave was dry and hot. "Quickly," he said, taking her hand.

They ran along the passageway. It sloped down, leading them deeper into this planet whose name was Chthon. Eons ago this twisting conduit had been formed by volcanic gases bubbling through molten rock; more recently, it had become a prison for those who were beyond redemption.

Aton ran swiftly with Malice by his side, and the dim-lit walls of the passageway seemed to drift past. There were no intersections or branches; no choice but to continue the way they were going. His chest began to ache, and fatigue started sapping his muscles. He forced himself on.

He rounded a corner and found that the passageway

opened into a large chamber. Its floor was littered with boulders. The ceiling receded into gloom.

It was a dead end. There was no way out.

He stopped and looked at Malice. Both of them were gasping for breath, their bodies filmed with sweat. Once again the shrieking sound reached them, louder than before, and the ground shook.

"There could be a small tunnel," she said, pointing to the tumble of rocks. "Hidden somewhere."

He nodded. "All right." Together they climbed from one boulder to another.

There was a rumbling sound, as of a human mob stampeding through the caverns. The rumbling grew louder. Aton turned to face the passageway through which they had just come. His stomach tightened reflexively. He scrambled higher, pulled Malice up beside him, and crouched behind an outcropping. "The light's very dim in here. It may not see us."

Suddenly the caterpillar was in the chamber. Huge faceted eyes swung slowly from side to side. The segments of its body—humanoid forms impaled like meat on a sinuous skewer—seemed to stir indecisively. It edged closer, and its eight-foot antennae brushed the walls.

One of them touched Malice on the shoulder. She cried out instinctively, unable to control her revulsion. She jumped up and tried to scramble around to the passageway that was the only exit from the cave.

It sensed her and turned with surprising speed. The long poisoned lance of its tail whipped around.

"No!" Aton shouted. He seized a rock and hurled it, aiming for one of the monster's bulbous eyes.

The caterpillar flipped protective bone shutters over its eyes as readily as a man might blink, and Aton's rock bounced harmlessly away. Still, he had distracted it at least temporarily: the beast was turning, focusing its dull mind on him now.

Malice seized the moment and leaped for the passageway out of the cave—but her foot slipped. There was a sound like the heel of a boot squelching into wet mud as she fell forward onto the beast's tail, and it sank deep into her abdomen.

Blood poured down her belly from the wound, and she struggled frantically. But within a few seconds the bleeding stopped as suddenly as it had begun, and her eyes glazed over as the poison spread through her. Her limbs went limp—and then, as Aton watched in horror, they stiffened and began to move in spastic imitation of the segments of the beast's body that had been speared before her.

"No!" Aton shouted again. He knew she was beyond help now, but he couldn't accept that fact. He tried to throw himself at the monster, to fight it with his bare hands. But his muscles no longer obeyed him. He watched, immobilized, as the creature turned and slowly shuffled out of the cavern, taking Malice with it. Her body receded from him, the limbs moving mechanically, the head nodding as if her neck had been broken.

Still Aton seemed paralyzed. He couldn't even breathe. This couldn't be happening; it was wrong. And with that thought came sudden release, as he woke to his bedroom on Hvee.

He took deep, shuddering breaths, staring up at the ceiling lit with gray morning light. He willed the horrifying images of Chthon from his mind. The dream had been so vivid, it hardly seemed like a dream at all. It seemed more like a message, or a prophecy.

He rolled over on the simple mattress padded with cotton and straw and looked for Malice beside him. The sheets were empty, and the pillow had not been touched. For a moment he felt confusion and concern, but then he remembered the previous night. There had been an argument. She had defied him. He had grown angry. Ultimately, he had shut her in the cellar. (The cellar—was this why he had dreamed of the underground prison of Chthon?)

Aton struggled out of bed and donned the simple peasant clothes that he normally wore while tending the fields of Hvee flowers. He moved easily, efficiently, his muscles strong from manual labor. His face was impassive, and he seemed calm; but his thoughts and feelings were in private turmoil.

Outside the small window, the fields of flowers were almost ready to be harvested. He paused a moment, trying to absorb the tranquillity of the scene as the sky turned gold with the first glow of sunlight and birds woke in the feathery leaves of the trees. Here was his home; he had spent his childhood in this house, had played with children at the nearby farms. True, it had not been a happy childhood; he had always sensed he was somehow different from the others. And yes, there had been a terrible truth to discover about himself—

He realized his thoughts were leading him inexorably back to his dream of Chthon. He shook his head, willing the images away. Surely he would feel better if he were with the woman he loved.

He paced quickly across the room, his tanned feet moving silently over wooden boards that gleamed with a deep, dark luster from centuries of use. He opened the door to the hallway.

He listened for a moment. His father, Aurelius, now slept in Aton's old room, while Aton had taken over his father's bedroom. The old man was probably still asleep. When he woke, he usually started calling for his breakfast.

Aton crept downstairs to the ground floor. The flagstones felt ice-cold under his feet and the morning air was cool on his bare arms. He walked along the hallway, past framed pictures of his forebears, and opened the door to the cellar.

He descended rough-hewn stone steps. The air here was rich with seasoned smells: chopped wood, hsin fruit individually wrapped and stored in crates for the winter months, dried herbs, bundles of fibers from rothp trees which Malice would spin into thread to weave new garments. She and he were self-sufficient in this little farmhouse.

He picked his way through a clutter of farm tools to a stout wooden door set in a stone wall that subdivided the cellar. He took a large, rusty key from a hook in the wall, turned it in the lock, and pushed the door open.

Faint light came from a tiny, grimy window up by the ceiling. It illuminated a floor of bare stone. In the center of it, a human figure lay huddled under a rough brown blanket.

Aton gently pulled the blanket down, revealing a tangle of red hair, a woman's face serene in sleep, her head pillowed on her arms. He touched her shoulder.

Malice stirred and rolled over. She looked up at him and blinked.

Aton felt irrational relief. The last aftertaste of his dream was banished by the sight of her here, alive. He realized, with discomfort, how much he needed and cared for her.

She winced as she felt the tenderness of his thought. Her telepathic intuition, shared by all the women from her world, inverted a man's emotions. His love she felt as hate; by contrast, when he felt angry and cruel, her senses translated these emotions into sweet romantic passion.

Aton deliberately suppressed his tender feelings. Still, he realized, he felt guilty about the punishment he had inflicted. "I shouldn't have left you down here last night," he said.

She studied his stern features for a moment, sensing the nuances of his emotional conflict. She sat up, and the blanket slid down, revealing her naked body. She ran her fingers through her hair, combing the tangles out of it. "Your punishment is my pleasure. You know that."

He brooded for a moment. "Our fights have been getting worse. My anger has been growing more extreme."

She smiled like a lover savoring an intimate caress. "Yes. I've noticed."

He gave her a vexed look. "I'm serious." He stood
and went to the small window. Outside, the morning
was bright, but it hardly seemed to penetrate the base-
ment gloom. Once again, the caves of Chthon seemed
to be hovering at the edges of his awareness. "There's
something wrong. Surely you've noticed it? I feel as if
we're on the edge of something ominous."

She shook her head. "I feel bored, that's all. Living
on this farm is boring. And frankly, listening to you
talking like this is boring." She pulled the blanket
around her body, as if withdrawing a gift she had been
willing to offer him a moment ago. She stood up to
leave.

He caught hold of her wrist. "I haven't finished."

She glanced at his hand gripping her, then looked
up at his face. Her expression was amused. "Are you
going to hold me here by force, just so that I have to
listen to your gloomy predictions? Now, that *would* be
a punishment."

The taunt stirred his anger, perhaps as it was meant
to. "What I'm saying is important."

"Really?" She gave her wrist a quick twist, wrenched
it free, and turned for the door.

He grabbed for her again—but found himself clutching only the blanket. She left him holding it and ran
naked up the stone steps. Her high, firm breasts quiv-
ered as she moved, and her muscles shifted under the
pale, perfect skin of her thighs. She didn't even bother
to look back.

Aton went after her. He caught up with her in the
kitchen. "Malice—"

"Oh, leave me alone." Her voice was cold. She
opened the door of the stove and put a log on the
embers that still glowed from the previous night. "You
know, I'm getting sick of living here." She poked
savagely at the fire. "I've even been thinking that
perhaps I should leave."

The words immobilized him for a moment. He stared
at her dumbly. Then his anger redoubled.

She looked at him, feeding on his emotions. "Ahh," she said, her eyes bright, her cheeks flushed.

"You said that just to provoke me."

"Maybe," she taunted him.

"Don't play with me," he warned her.

"Oh, do you think I'm playing?" She tilted her chin up provocatively. Her back had straightened and her nipples had stiffened. She was high on his growing rage.

He reached out quickly to grab her arm—but she pulled back and he found himself stumbling, grappling with empty air. The indignity of it made him angrier than ever.

"You're getting slow," she taunted him. "Do you realize that? Slow and stupid. It must be because you spend all your time living on this farm where nothing happens. Your mind's going dead. I saw the same thing happen to Aurelius."

"Don't talk like that about my father!" He tried again to grab her, but she skipped to one side, keeping just out of reach.

"You don't like to think about me and him, do you?" She gave him a strange, malicious smile.

"Bitch!" He stepped forward and swung his arm, and this time she wasn't fast enough. He slapped her face, and her head rocked back. She gasped, but whether it was in pain or pleasure was hard to tell. Her cheek turned slowly pink, showing the outline of his fingers. Then her dangerous smile returned. "Your father used to hit me harder than that."

Aton grabbed both her arms in his and threw her to the floor. He paused, breathing hard, dizzy with rage and passion. Quickly, he ripped his clothes off; and then he fell on her.

She struggled at first, as if she needed to test his strength before she would submit to it. They wrestled on the flagstones, grunting and gasping, and then she fell backward against the wood-burning stove and cried out in pain. He hardly noticed, and he didn't care. He forced himself on her, and at last she surrendered to him. She closed her eyes, feeding on his cruel emotions, and he didn't release her until his passion was spent.

A little later, she was in his arms, gasping for breath. She wrapped her arms around his neck, pressed close, and kissed him long and hard. Her body moved languorously against him, then slowly subsided. Bright red marks disfigured her skin where the stove had burned her.

He touched the marks and shook his head in confusion, shocked by his own violence. "I hurt you," he said.

She smiled lazily. "Yes."

"No, I really hurt you. Do you need—"

She gestured dismissively. "It was nothing."

He looked more closely and saw that it was true. The burn marks were already fading. Her body was the product of the same experiment in genetic engineering that had enhanced her intuition and scrambled her emotions. Her skin had inhuman resilience and ability to heal itself.

Aton helped her up onto a chair, then sat beside her. He rested his elbows on the kitchen table, feeling drained and dizzy. "It could have been much worse," he said. "I didn't know what I was doing."

She put her arm around his shoulders and kissed his cheek. "I wouldn't have been satisfied with anything less."

"But *every day*? And you need more each time."

She shrugged. "There really isn't much else to do here." She paused, and her green eyes shifted. "You know," she went on, sounding more thoughtful, "we should go someplace for a vacation. I'd enjoy a change of scenery."

He nodded mechanically. "Of course. As soon as the harvest is in."

"Oh, yes. The harvest." She stood up, and her look

of sensual satisfaction gradually faded. "I suppose I should make Aurelius his breakfast."

Aton turned and looked up at her, trying to read her expression. "You know, when you spoke of leaving—"

She placed a skillet on the stove. "Did you really wonder if I meant it?"

He nodded.

She took a long, pink, tubular vegetable from a storage cupboard and laid it on a cutting board, her fingers moving thoughtfully over its rounded form. "You'll never lose me, Aton," she said, picking up a knife. "Not so long as you give me what I need."

2.

He walked out into the soft, cool morning. The air was full of the sweet smell of Hvee flowers, and the sky was a hazy lavender-gray as the pale sun edged above the hills at the horizon.

Small feet came scampering through the dirt. A furry shape launched itself toward Aton, and eager little paws grabbed at his clothing. He glanced down at what looked like a brown rug wrapping itself around his waist and thighs. A little black face peered up from a mess of tufty hair. "Aton?" The voice was high-pitched and not quite human. "Hug?"

He hauled it up to his chest. The creature grinned and wrapped its six arms around him, chittering happily. It was an emp, from a low-gravity forest world where most animals spent their entire lives in the trees. Its thin, flat body enabled it to glide like a flying squirrel. Its extra pair of paws enabled it to swing easily from branch to branch. Here on Hvee, however, the gravity was higher, and the emp did most of its traveling draped across Aton's back.

It made an ideal pet. It was always friendly, and soaked up human affection. Alix, a woman who owned one of the neighboring farms, had brought it to Hvee and given it to Aton. As time went by, to his surprise, he'd grown to like the way it hung around him.

As for Alix, she hung around him, too. During the last few months, she'd made it quietly obvious that she was available if he wanted an affair with her. She was shy where Malice was bold. She was undemanding where Malice was challenging and provocative. She was slender and graceful—and Aton was tempted.

But he cut the thought off. An affair with a woman who had normal emotional responses was out of the question for him. His fits of rage could be physically dangerous. That was the legacy of his genes, and there was no escape from it, now or ever.

In a grim frame of mind, he lifted the emp up onto his shoulders and walked across the yard to the pen where he kept chickens imported from Old Earth. They were strutting and bickering, impatient to be fed. He realized that allowing himself to be seduced by Malice had delayed his morning schedule. She didn't seem to understand that chores on a farm couldn't be postponed according to whim, especially around harvest time. Or maybe she did understand, but preferred not to.

Aton dumped the chicken feed into the bins. He turned back toward the house. Six months ago, when he had returned here to settle with the woman he loved, he had felt total fulfillment of a kind he had never believed possible. Why did nothing seem to please him now? And why did the future now seem so unknown and threatening?

When he entered the kitchen he found that the table had been set for breakfast and pots were simmering on the stove, but Malice was nowhere to be seen. Aton started across the flagstones toward the front hall, then thought better of it and sat down in one of the sturdy pegged-wood chairs. He put the emp on the floor. "Stay," he told it.

It made a petulant clucking noise and sidled under his chair. It blinked its big eyes at him and tucked its paws under its furry body, rolling itself into a little ball. "Food?" it asked hopefully.

"Soon," said Aton. "I think."

A moment later Malice walked in, now dressed in home-woven work clothes. The shirt was a tight fit, clearly revealing the shape of her breasts. Her eyes

were bright and her cheeks were pink. The abuse that
she had received from him obviously had had no last-
ing ill-effects. On the contrary, it had revitalized her.

"Where were you?" he asked her.

"Feeding Aurelius." She gave him a strange, ambig-
uous look, then walked to the stove. "I suppose you're
ready for breakfast?"

"Of course." He hesitated. "How is my father?"

"The same." She met his eyes, then looked away.
He couldn't tell whether there was something that she
wasn't saying, or whether it was just his imagination.
Her relationship with his father was a topic that they
never discussed.

They ate mostly in silence. Aton listed the jobs that
needed to be done that day, and Malice quietly agreed.

The emp eventually became restless, crawled out
from under Aton's chair, and tried to hoist itself onto
his leg in pursuit of the tempting breakfast smells.
Aton smiled and gave it a scrap of bread. It clasped
the morsel in its front paws and gnawed on it. "Good,"
it said.

"Please," said Malice. She looked pained.

"I'm sorry," said Aton. "I forgot." He scooped the
emp up, took it to the back door, and put it outside.
Malice didn't object to the creature itself, only to the
warm feelings of affection that it roused in him. To
her inverted telepathic senses, those feelings were painful and physically damaging. He knew that; so why
had he brought the emp inside to begin with? To hurt
her in a way that physical abuse never could?

3.

Aton was riding out into the fields when he saw the hovercar. It was turning off the dirt road at the top of the hill, nosing into the narrow, overgrown track that led down to the house. Its fans raised a wake of dust, and it fishtailed as it encountered potholes and ruts in the track. The driver seemed to be having trouble maintaining control.

Aton dismounted from his hrule and tethered it back by the barn. The big animal looked like a skinny, oversize, long-legged bear. It was native to Hvee, and its docile temperament suited it to farm work. It watched impassively as he walked out to the graveled semicircle in front of the house and stood there, waiting.

The emp scampered over and climbed up onto his shoulders so that it could get a better view. Visitors were rare—Aton discouraged them—and vehicles were virtually unknown. The aristocracy that owned and governed the planet made sure of that.

The car finally reached the open area in front of the house, and the driver cut its power. It drifted to a halt, sinking slowly as the air cushion deflated.

The man who got out was pink, plump, and bald, wearing a white shirt and a caramel suit. His brown shoes were shiny and his tie was tightly knotted. He hitched up his pants, glanced at the Hvee fields, then waddled around the car toward Aton. His thick lips widened in a cheerful grin. "Nice day," he said. He nodded as if inviting Aton to agree with him.

Aton regarded the man skeptically. He looked like a salesman. "Can I help you?"

"I'm looking for an Aurelius Five." The fat man grinned some more. "Does he still own this farm?"

Aton shook his head. "He's my father. I run the place now."

"Ah. Ah, well, then, you're the one I need to see." He held out his hand. "My name's Schenck. I'm from offworld. Just came in yesterday, left my ship at the landing field outside the village." He spoke awkwardly, as if he had some kind of speech impediment that slurred his voice. "I'm a trader. When I was here last year, I bought a large part of the harvest from your father."

Aton forced a polite smile. Business, after all, was business. He shook the man's hand. "I'm pleased to meet you, Mr. Schenck. I'm Aton Five."

Schenck saw the emp peeking at him from behind Aton's shoulder. "Well, what have we here?" He extended a finger to tickle it under its chin. "Hey, little fellow."

"No." The emp's voice was a startled squeak. The furry animal dropped suddenly to the ground, ran to the house, and swarmed up the wall, sharp claws clinging to fissures between the stones. It swung up over the gutter, then climbed to the top of the roof and sat there chattering like a monkey.

"What's its problem?" said Schenck, looking vaguely irritated.

"It isn't accustomed to strangers. Not many people come here."

"Hm." Schenck shrugged. "Well, I would like to inspect your crop, to see what you've got. Maybe we can make a deal, eh?"

"I'll be glad to show you around," said Aton.

They took Schenck's car along the dirt track that ran around the perimeter of the farm. The acres of Hvee blossoms rippled in the wind, a dazzling carpet of green. Schenck talked vaguely about nothing in particular while his eyes darted busily from side to side, taking in every detail.

"You've improved the land," he observed. "Must have worked hard."

"Yes," said Aton. "I have."

"So what is the story with your father?" Schenck asked, as he finally turned the car back toward the house.

"He's not very well."

"Very sick?" Schenck's eyes were half hidden by folds of plump flesh, making his face hard to read.

"Swamp fever, from more than twenty years ago," said Aton. "I'm sure you noticed when you were here last year—he wasn't in good health then."

"He seemed a bit pale," Schenck agreed.

"In the past few months he's become much worse. The local doctor has no idea what's wrong."

Schenck frowned. "No idea? Why not?"

"Hvee imposes high tariffs on any imported hardware. It's our way of maintaining the unspoiled, rustic life-style. But it means we lack modern medical equipment."

"Well, now," said Schenck, "I have a portable med unit." He gestured with his thumb to the rear storage compartment. "Never travel without it. I'll run a diagnosis for you, no problem at all. Glad to be able to help."

"Thank you," Aton said slowly. He wondered why Schenck's offer didn't seem more welcome.

Back at the house, they climbed the stairs to Aurelius's bedroom. "Father?" Aton knocked on the door. He opened it slowly.

The room had a musty, dusty smell. The old man was lying in bed with his head turned to one side, staring out the window at the fields. His body was a thin shape under the hand-embroidered quilt, and his face was pale, deeply mapped with a network of fine lines.

"Father," Aton said, "I have someone to see you."

Aurelius turned his head slowly. He looked at Aton, then at Schenck, but his expression never changed, and there was a distant look in his eyes.

"Mr. Aurelius Five." Schenck beamed at him. "Good day to you, sir." He set the med unit on the bed and opened its carrying case. "Perhaps you remember me."

The old man slowly blinked. He said nothing.

"Don't take it personally," said Aton. "He's like this with everyone."

"Too bad, too bad." Schenck broke open a blister-pack and attached a sterile tip to the unit's probe. He took Aurelius's arm, lying on the covers, and touched the probe briefly to the withered skin.

For a moment, there was silence in the little room, broken only by the slow ticking of an old pendulum clock that stood by the door. One dial on its face showed the planting and harvesting seasons for Hvee flowers; another displayed the time on the two other colonized planets in the system.

The med unit chimed. Schenck removed its probe, leaving a tiny dot of blood. He studied the unit's readout. "Swamp fever, yes. And—" He paused, frowning. "Another possible contagion, unspecified. Unspecified?" He seemed puzzled. He shook his head. "Perhaps an offworld virus?"

"Aurelius hasn't left this planet in the past twenty years," said Aton.

Schenck shrugged. He discarded the probe tip and slid the unit back into its case. "Then I really don't know. Mr. Aurelius, may you get well soon." He leaned forward and patted the old man's bony shoulder with his pink, plump hand.

A look of distant recognition seemed to flicker briefly in Aurelius's eyes, and his mouth twitched in a bare hint of a smile. But then he turned his head away. He sighed deeply as he stared once more out the window at the fields of flowers.

Aton walked Schenck out of the house, back to his car. "Thank you for your trouble," he said, as Schenck

opened the door and eased himself into the driving
seat.

"No trouble, no trouble at all." He put the med unit
on the seat beside him. "I will be back tomorrow, Mr.
Aton Five, with an offer. You see, I have other farms
to inspect before I can say anything definite." He
grinned again, and Aton saw something devious in the
man's eyes. He decided he didn't like Schenck; didn't
trust him at all.

Schenck reached for the switch to start the car, then
paused, staring ahead through the windshield. "Your
wife?" he asked.

Malice was walking toward the house, hauling water
from the well in two wooden buckets hanging from a
yoke across her shoulders. The load was heavy and
she moved slowly, treading carefully. Her breasts trembled under her tight clothes as she took each step.

"Yes," Aton said. "My wife."

"Strength and beauty," mused Schenck. "Yes indeed." He pursed his lips thoughtfully. "Once before,
I saw a woman like that. The red hair, the physical
strength. Planet Minion? Yes, yes, that was the place."
He turned and looked up inquiringly at Aton.

"Appearances can be deceptive." Aton calmly returned the man's stare. "Malice was born right here
on Hvee."

"Malice? Unusual name." Schenck watched her some
more, until she moved out of sight behind the house.
"But if she was from Minion she could not be here,
could she? Minion is a Proscribed world, as I recall.
No one is allowed in, and no one is allowed out.
Federation law."

Aton shrugged. "I wouldn't know. I've never heard
of the place."

"No?" Schenck chuckled. "Strange people. Yes indeed, very strange social customs and genetic history."
He switched on his car's motor.

Aton stepped back as the vehicle lifted, stirring

dust. He watched as Schenck turned it and drove
slowly away along the track. When he reached the
road, he turned toward the village. The car crested the
hill and finally disappeared from view.

4.

The mallet made a regular, heavy smacking sound as he hammered the post into the thick, dark soil. He paused, breathing deeply, and flexed his shoulders. A grove of feather-fronded trees shaded him from the afternoon sun, but he was hot nevertheless. He looked at the emp, lazily batting its paw at an insect buzzing past, and his hrule, grazing contentedly on grass at the edge of the Hvee field. The animals, as usual, seemed to be having the easier time of it.

"Aton?" The voice came from behind him, amid the trees.

He turned quickly with all his muscles suddenly tense. He realized that his nerves had been on edge since Schenck had left. Or maybe since his nightmare that morning. "Who is it?"

She emerged from the shadows. "Alix. I'm sorry, did I startle you?" she gave him a shy smile. She was tall and slim, dressed in work clothes that she'd evidently brought with her from offworld: khaki pants, leather boots, and a gingham shirt that she'd knotted under her breasts, leaving her waist bare. Her hair was brown, parted in the center, and it hung straight to her shoulders. She looked at Aton with soft brown eyes. "I saw you working out here, so I brought you something to drink," she said. "I thought maybe on a hot day like this, you'd be thirsty." She handed him a tall glass of water. Ice tinkled in it.

"Thanks." He took it from her. "You shouldn't have troubled."

29

"It's no trouble." She walked over and squatted by the emp. "Hi, little fellow. Is Aton taking good care of you?"

"Alix." The emp recognized her easily enough, but had trouble pronouncing her name. It nuzzled her hand. "Happy," it said, flopping back into the grass.

"That's good." She petted it for a moment, then turned back to Aton. "What are you doing?"

"Rebuilding the fence. The posts were rotten."

She looked at his tanned, naked chest. "Sounds like a dull job. I guess it's good for building muscles. I mean, not that you need any more than you've already got." She laughed self-consciously.

He drained the glass and handed it back to her. Momentarily, their fingers touched and their eyes met.

"Everything all right at your place?" he asked politely.

She shrugged. "Sure. I've finally settled in." She had arrived on Hvee only four months before.

She fell silent, standing awkwardly in front of him as if there was something she wanted to say, but she didn't know how to say it.

Aton watched her steadily. "Is there something wrong?"

She avoided his eyes. "Not really."

"Tell me, Alix."

"Well, I'd kind of like it if you felt like stopping by sometime."

Gently, he touched her cheek. She seemed so vulnerable. He found it almost unbearably seductive. He imagined holding her. She wouldn't resist, he knew that. He had the sense that she would yield to him completely. He would possess her, and she would let him do anything he wanted. But there, that was the trap. Sooner or later her compliant nature would tempt him into losing control—maybe just for a few moments. He would hurt her. It was inevitable.

"Alix, there are reasons—ones I can't explain to

you now—that I can never be more than your neighbor. Maybe not even your friend."

"I—realize you're married."

"That's not what I'm talking about. There are things about me that you don't know." He felt a heaviness in his chest. It was hard, very hard, pushing her away from him. "If you knew more about me, you might not want to know me at all."

"I doubt that." Her brown eyes seemed soft and understanding, and for a strange moment he felt as if she knew everything about him, and still accepted him, despite it all.

She moved quickly toward him and kissed him quickly on the cheek. Then she turned and made her way back toward the woods. "If you ever change your mind," she called to him, "let me know."

Aton imagined holding her. She was so slender, so delicate.

The thought made him aroused. He swore, turned, and picked up the mallet. He raised it and brought it down with all his strength, pounding the fence post into the soil.

5.

When he walked into the house at the end of the day, it seemed dark and deserted. He lit an oil lamp in the kitchen and another in the hallway. "Malice?" he called. There was no reply.

He felt the same sense of foreboding that had gripped him in the morning. It made him angry; he was not superstitious, and he didn't believe in premonitions. But still something seemed *wrong*.

He walked slowly up the stairs. Faintly, he heard voices. They seemed to come from Aurelius's room.

He pushed the door open. In the last dim light from the setting sun he saw Malice sitting on the bed, leaning over the old man. Aurelius had been muttering something, and it looked as if she had been leaning close to hear him.

She turned quickly. "What do you want?" She sounded impatient.

"I—wondered where you were."

"Leave us alone for a few minutes," she told him. "Please."

"Why?" he asked.

"It's important."

He hesitated. "All right." He closed the door.

Downstairs, he sat in the kitchen. The heat of the day had gone, and the air felt cool. He opened the door of the stove and stared into the embers. He tried to think of nothing as he watched the patterns in the fire. Nothing at all.

She joined him a little later. "I'm sorry I snapped at

you," she said. She touched the back of his neck, then
his cheek.

He looked at her warily. "What was going on in
there?"

"Just talking about—old times. Are you hungry?"
She said it vaguely, as if she was finding it hard to
concentrate. She picked up a saucepan, then put it
down.

"Of course I'm hungry," he said. "But I want to
know what's going on." He walked over, took her
wrist, and turned her to face him.

"Nothing." Her eyes seemed unfocused. "Nothing
that concerns you."

He sighed, exasperated. "Look—" He broke off.
There had been a strange noise from upstairs.

He paused, listening. There was a distant coughing,
choking noise, and a throttled cry.

Aton turned and ran out of the kitchen. He leaped
up the stairs to Aurelius's room and threw open the
door.

The old man was sitting up in bed with an expression of surprise. His mouth was gaping wide. His
breath came in rattling gasps. He saw Aton and reached
out toward him. His hand was trembling.

Aton strode forward. He put his arm around his
father. The man's body felt impossibly bony and thin.
His head rolled back and he stared up into Aton's
face. "Kill you," he gasped. He swallowed hard, and
his chest shook. He tried to take a breath, but started
to choke again, as if his throat was blocked. His whole
body convulsed.

Aton slapped him between the shoulder blades, then
moved behind the old man and wrapped him arms
around his stomach. He clenched the fist of one hand
and cupped the other around it. He pulled in hard,
squeezing Aurelius's abdomen. He did it again, and
Aurelius leaned forward and vomited.

In the dim gray light from outside, it was hard to see

what was happening. Dark liquid splashed onto the sheets. There was a strange, foul smell of decay.

Aurelius took a shaky breath. He turned his head. "She," he whispered. "She—"

"Try to relax," Aton told him. "Lie down, Father. Deep breaths."

But the old man went into another convulsion. He wrenched free from Aton's grip and flopped onto his side, drawing his knees up to his chest. He vomited again—and this time the flow seemed endless, as if someone had opened a faucet. Gallons of the thick, black, sludgy liquid gushed out of his mouth. The liquid pooled in the bed, overflowed, and ran onto the floor.

Aton drew back, dazed with horror. The old man lay there with his eyes closed and his mouth gaping wide. The liquid poured out of him, more and more of it, in a torrent.

Aton turned and saw Malice standing in the doorway. "He's dying," he said. "My father's dying."

She shook her head. Her expression was unreadable. "He is already dead."

6.

Aton carried an oil lamp into the room that had once been Aurelius's study. He felt dazed, detached from the world, as if it no longer involved him. The shadows cast by the lamp flickered and jumped. In the wavering light he saw a big old desk, made by his grandfather; books neatly stacked on metal shelves; a wooden globe; family holos in ornate frames; leather-upholstered furniture filmed with dust. The room smelled musty and dead.

On an end table stood a model of the starship that had brought Aton's ancestors to Hvee five generations ago. He ran his fingers briefly over the tapered cylinder, then set down the lamp and turned his attention to a modern shortwave transceiver standing nearby.

The unit hadn't been used in months. He checked the batteries; they were still good. He entered a code on the keypad, then listened with numb detachment to the ringing tone. Upstairs he could hear Malice's footsteps as she cleaned up the mess in Aurelius's bedroom.

"Hello?" The voice came from the transceiver's loudspeaker.

Aton blinked. "Dr. Wolk?"

"Yes, this is Wolk."

He struggled for words. "I—my father's dead." That sounded clear enough, yet wrong, as if it couldn't possibly be true.

"What's that?" Wolk had been the village physician for the past fifty years. He was no longer entirely competent, but there was no one to replace him.

35

"My father!" Aton shouted into the handset. "Please come at once. It's an emergency."

Wolk muttered something that sounded like an acknowledgment. He was one of the few people in the area who owned any form of transportation. It was a broken-down ground car with bald tires and only one headlight, but it would get him to the house within a half-hour.

Aton switched off the transceiver, picked up the oil lamp, and walked back upstairs. He found Malice using a shovel to scoop thick black gunk off the floor and into a wooden bucket. She had opened all the windows to get rid of the foul smell. Aurelius was still lying on his side with his legs drawn up, his eyes shut, his mouth gaping wide.

Aton touched his father's face. The skin buckled under his fingers as if there were no longer any bones beneath. A gentle breeze wafted in through the open windows, and the old man's corpse stirred like a dry husk. Aton drew back, feeling his stomach clench. As he watched, Aurelius's body slowly crumpled in on itself, as if it were made of flimsy paper. A rotten odor came out of his mouth.

"Help me strip the bed." Malice looked at Aton and waited.

Dumbly, he did what she asked. The covers were saturated with the thick black liquid. She rolled them quickly into a ball.

"Bring the buckets," she told him, as she carried the bedding out of the room.

He picked them up and followed her downstairs, through the dim-lit hallway, out into the backyard. "Where are you going?"

"We should dump everything in the cesspit. It could be contaminated."

"If it is, then so are we." But still, he did as she suggested.

Back in the house, he realized he was trembling. He looked at the smears of black stuff on his hands. "I don't want to go back up there," he told her in a low voice.

"Why not?"

He laughed, feeling crazy with the horror of what he'd seen. "Why not? He's my *father*."

She looked at him for a moment. Her face was expressionless. "Not anymore. He's dead, now."

Aton stared at her. "Yes, that's right. I saw. I was there, remember? I was holding him in my arms." He drew a shaky breath. "If you want to make it all neat and clean, you go ahead." He turned away—then turned back. "What were you talking about with him, before he started choking?"

She seemed to think for a moment before answering. "We were talking, that's all."

"About what? Why did you tell me to leave you alone with him?"

"It was private. It was about the past." Her eyes lost their intent focus. "I loved him too. Once."

Aton went into the kitchen. He slumped onto a chair and rested his elbows on the table. He felt unbalanced. The world seemed suddenly strange and hostile. He no longer trusted anyone or anything. Not Malice, not Schenck—definitely not Schenck. The man had used his med unit on Aurelius. It had made a tiny puncture in the old man's skin. Was that significant? Or maybe Aton himself was to blame. Maybe he was carrying some offworld disease, was a vector for a virus that might kill him next, or Malice—

He got up and walked out of the house, into the Hvee fields. The emp came creeping through the darkness and made an inquisitive noise. "Hug?" it said.

Aton stooped and picked up the little animal. It hugged him; he hugged it back. He stood there for a long time, staring up at the stars.

7.

He heard whining motors and the dull groaning of wheel bearings in need of oil. Aton turned and saw Dr. Wolk's car bumping along the track toward the house, its single headlight beam flickering yellow. It shuddered to a halt and Wolk climbed out. "All right," he said without any preliminaries. "What's this about an emergency?"

"My father," Aton said. His thoughts had quietened, leaving a strange dull indifference. "He's dead."

Wolk grunted. "You sure?"

Aton nodded. "Completely sure."

Wolk sighed. "Was afraid he was getting weaker. God knows, I've been doing what I could."

"You have no reason to feel any blame," Aton said. He put the emp down and led the way into the house.

Malice came out of Aurelius's room onto the landing when she heard Wolk make his way slowly up the stairs. She was holding a scrubbing brush. There was a strong smell of soap. "Why did you call a doctor here?" she asked Aton. "It's far too late for him to do anything."

"I'll decide that, young lady." Wolk glared at her and moved arthritically into Aurelius's room.

The body on the mattress had collapsed completely and was now a flat wrinkled shape like a deflated balloon. Wolk muttered something, picked up the oil lamp, and peered closer. When he prodded Aurelius's dead skin it made dry crinkling noises under his touch.

He stepped back with a little sound of disgust. He

38

turned toward Aton, his eyeglasses glittering in the lamplight. "What the hell happened here?"

"I heard him choking," Aton explained. "There seemed to be something in his throat. I tried to force it up. He was trying to say something." Aton remembered his father's fragmented words, but some cautious instinct prevented him from mentioning them. "He started vomiting. It went on and on. Black gunk, flowing out of him—"

"What happened to this black stuff?"

"I cleaned it up." Malice spoked from behind them.

"All of it?" Wolk turned and scowled at her. "We could use a sample. Analyze it."

Aton doubted Wolk's ability to analyze anything more challenging than a urine sample, but he said nothing.

Malice shrugged. "I'm sorry. I disposed of it."

Wolk grunted. He surveyed Aurelius's body again, and shook his head. "Never seen anything like this. You two were offworld till six months ago, isn't that right?"

"We were blood-tested and tissue-scanned by a diagnostic system before we landed," Malice said calmly. "It didn't find any microorganisms."

"Could be it made a mistake."

"If we were incubating an offworld virus," Malice went on, "and then we passed it to Aurelius, it should have affected us before it affected him."

Wolk shook his head. "Can never tell." He walked out of the room. "Have to call the authorities." He started down the stairs. "Maybe quarantine you. Don't touch the body, understand? I'll call you in the morning."

8.

"The man who came to the house today," Aton said, as he pulled his clothes off. "Schenck. Did you see him?"

Malice shook her head. She was lying in bed with her eyes closed. She'd hardly spoken since the doctor had left.

Aton sat on the mattress beside her. "Well, he saw you. You were carrying water from the well."

"What of it?" She sounded sleepy and uninterested.

"He guessed where you were from. I denied it, but I'm not sure if he believed me. It was hard to tell. I didn't trust him."

She shrugged one shoulder. She said nothing.

"You know, he had a med unit with him. He used it on Aurelius. It seems a strange coincidence—"

"You think anyone who comes here is going to try and hurt us in some way. You think the world is full of enemies." She sighed. "That's why no one ever visits us."

"We have good reason to be cautious," he said defensively. "You *are* from a Proscribed world."

For a moment she was silent, as if trying carefully to decide what to say. Finally she turned her head to look at him. "Sometimes I wonder," she said, "if you're really the man I thought I knew."

He sat there, close to her but not touching her, and tried to understand. "All I want—" he began.

She sat up, roused from her drowsiness by her own impatience. "All you want is to hide from anything

40

that might hurt you. You'd like to spend the rest of your life plowing the fields and hugging that stupid animal that hugs you back."

He felt a twinge of irritation. "Are you trying to annoy me? Didn't you get enough abuse this morning?"

She laughed loudly. She stared at him with a strange, wild light in her eyes. "Oh, no. Sex is the last thing I want from you now." She paused for a moment in order to sample the conflicting emotions she had roused in him. "I suppose I may as well tell you," she went on. She tossed her long hair aside, and leaned closer, staring directly into his face. "I'm pregnant. Do you hear me, Aton? Do you understand what that means?"

9.

He stumbled barefoot through the darkness, naked from the waist up. The chill night air clutched his chest and arms. His feet were wet with dew.

He zigzagged through the Hvee fields, trampling the blossoms. Memories flickered before him: a red-haired, green-eyed woman in a forest glade, seducing a seven-year-old boy with a kiss; the same woman in a small modern room with plastic furnishings, telling him a secret about himself that filled him with self-loathing and inarticulate rage; the woman again, a little later, in a wooden cabin on the planet Minion, tantalizing him with her body and handing him a whip with which to defile it . . .

He saw a house, and stumbled toward it. There was a lamp burning in a window, and a woman sitting reading a leather-bound book. Aton made his way to the glass and peered in, wondering stupidly if he had traveled in a circle and returned to his own home. But this woman was brown-haired, and her face showed a gentle softness; she was quite different from Malice, the woman he loved.

He banged his hand against the glass, and she turned quickly, startled by the sound. She saw him standing there, and her expression changed. She smiled uncertainly, put down the book, and hurried from the room.

The front door of the house opened. Light flooded out. "Aton! Is it you?"

He blundered in and stood in the hallway, breathing hard. "Alix." He stared at her, searching for words.

She noted his disheveled hair, his bare chest, the crushed Hvee blossoms sticking to his wet bare feet. "What's happened? What's wrong?"

"My father died. Tonight."

"Oh. Oh, Aton." She closed the front door. "Here. Come into the living room." She took his arm.

He tried to pull away from her. She was wearing nothing but a thin nightdress. He could see the shape of her breasts through it, the dark circles of her nipples, the shadow of her pubis. "No," he muttered.

"You obviously need someone to talk to. Come and sit down." She tugged at his arm again, and this time, reluctantly, he followed.

"I shouldn't be here," he told her.

"Sit." She pushed him gently onto the couch. "I'm glad you're here." She went out into the kitchen.

"You're a kind person," he said. He let his head fall back, and his eyes closed. "Nothing bad must happen to you, Alix."

"Why should it?" Out in the kitchen, there was the sound of a spoon stirring something in a cup.

"My wife—" Aton began.

Alix came back in. "I want you to tell me about it, but drink this first." She handed him a cup of hot liquid. "It's a remedy."

"For what?"

She sat down opposite him. "I'm a botanist. Or I was, before I decided to come here and farm Hvee flowers. I know about herbal remedies."

He smelled the brew, and decided that he might as well drink it. It couldn't hurt, and it might even help.

"Now tell me everything."

He stared for a moment at her body. She looked infinitely desirable. Deliberately, he looked away. "You think talking will help?"

"It'll help me to understand. Then maybe I can help you. Go back to the very beginning, Aton." She made herself more comfortable in her chair. "You were born here on Hvee, weren't you?"

10.

I was born (Aton began) in the same house where I live now. Supposedly, my mother died in childbirth. Immediately afterward, my father left and went traveling, to try to heal the emotional wounds. On an alien world he met a beautiful woman, fell in love, and brought her back here. But their romance was short-lived, and she left him. He remained alone, after that.

When I was seven, I was playing in the forest. I heard a woman singing—the sweetest, most beautiful song. I found her sitting in a glade, and she called me to her as if she had known I would come. She picked a wild Hvee flower and gave it to me, and she told me I would never meet another woman as beautiful as she was. She kissed me. It was a strange, exquisite experience. It haunted me for years afterward.

When I was fourteen, again I heard the song. I found her in the same clearing in the forest, looking exactly as I remembered her. She . . . toyed with me. And then dismissed me. I still had no idea who she was.

When I was twenty-one, my father arranged a marriage for me with a daughter of Four. It would have been an honor to marry up one social level; but I wouldn't hear of it. I was fixated on the woman I had seen in the glade. And once again I heard her song. But this time, when I got there, she was gone. There was a word scratched into the fallen leaves: MALICE.

My father warned me that she was from the planet Minion. He made her sound like a myth-figure—the siren who lures men and enslaves them with a kiss. In reality, she was the cloned product of a gene-splice that didn't take. It was supposed to produce the ultimate female sex object, every man's fantasy of a courtesan. It succeeded—but it failed. Minionettes are virtually immortal, and show no signs of age. They are strong and immune to small injuries. But they have an inverted telepathic sense. They can only feel passion and love with a man who is full of pain and hate. Conversely, they are crippled by affection; a man who loves his wife can kill her.

The Federation placed Minion off-limits, as a Proscribed world. But the woman in the glade evaded the prohibition, and I became obsessed with her. I joined the space navy and traveled through the galaxy. I located her, in the end, because she wanted me to. Only then did she tell me who she really was.

She was my mother. The woman my father had married did indeed die in childbirth—but her baby died also. When my father left home after that, he met Malice on Minion and brought her back to Hvee. *That* was when I was born. I was a half-breed, although I didn't know it. I carry Minion genes—and some of the Minion sickness. My feelings toward women are a terrible mixture of sentiment and cruelty. A Minionette feeds on my rage; any normal woman is victimized by it. I'm liable to hurt and maybe even kill the person who loves me.

My father was no half-breed; he had normal tender feelings. He loved Malice—so she left him, before his love could kill her. Still, she couldn't resist coming back every seven years to see me, her son. And—she seduced me.

On Minion, you see, a woman's first child is always a boy. If her husband leaves, or grows old, her son grows up to take his place. A Minionette lives many times as long as a Minion man, remember. So she takes up with her son; and then, as he grows older, she conceives a new son with him and repeats the pattern. Only when she nears the end of her long life does she conceive a female child to replace herself.

So I was confronted with a terrible truth: that the woman whom I longed for, and finally found, was my mother, who had obsessed my father before me. And although this filled me with shame and self-loathing, there was no escape—for I shared the sickness of her heritage.

11.

Aton fell silent and looked away, uneasy at having told her so many secrets of his life. "Perhaps you see now why I've tried to avoid you," he said.

She stood up, walked to him, and took the empty cup out of his hands. She placed it on a table, then sat at the opposite end of the couch. She seemed calm, as if nothing he had said had shocked her. "You have no reason to sound so ashamed. You were born as you are. You had no choice."

"It's a stigma." Aton grimaced as if the words themselves tasted bad. "When I first learned the truth, I took out my rage on anyone and anything around me." He looked toward the window, at the blackness outside. "I could have stayed on that path. I could have rejected Malice and given myself up to the sadism in me. I would have killed for pleasure; they would have imprisoned me, in the end, and sometimes I dream about that, as if there's another universe where it actually happened, and I'm condemned to an underworld of caverns . . ."

"But that didn't happen," said Alix. She reached for Aton's hand and held it in hers, as if trying to anchor him in the present time, with her. "Tell me what happened after you learned that you were Malice's son, and you decided to stay with her."

He shrugged. "All right. We went secretly to Minion, despite the prohibition against anyone leaving or visiting the planet. I wanted to see the world she came from. But—my presence there was discovered. We were apprehended and shipped off to Federation head-quarters on Luna, the moon of Old Earth.

"I became involved in a crisis facing people there. They had learned of an alien entity, an inhuman plasma intelligence which they detected living at the center of Chthon, the prison planet. Largely through my efforts, we destroyed it. And I liberated the people who had been imprisoned in the caves of Chthon. They live on its surface now.*

"After that, the people of Luna invited me to return there. But I thought I had come to terms with my love for Malice, and I wanted a chance to achieve the fulfillment I had never had before. Also, I wanted to tell my father that I had found out everything, and could forgive him. I knew he was sick, and he might not live long. So I came here with Malice just six months ago. For a while, it worked."

"Until tonight?"

He shook his head slowly. "I think from the beginning, she resented my happiness here. A Minionette needs pain and rage in her husband, and she'll provoke it if she has to. Of course, in a sense, I needed that myself—some of the time. But tonight—tonight, she told me she's pregnant." He turned and gave Alix a searching, intense look. "You realize the implications?"

She shook her head.

"She's decided that it's time to replace me, just as she once conceived me to replace my father before me, when she realized his love made it impossible for her to stay with him."

"Oh." Alix sighed. "I see."

Aton drew a deep breath and let it out slowly. "But none of this is your concern. Alix, you've been kind to listen to me. But I should go now."

"No." She said the word firmly, and tightened her grip on his hand. "I won't let you leave here tonight."

He shook his head. "It isn't wise."

*Author's note: As described in *Plasm*.

She reached out with her other hand and combed her fingers through his hair, then ran them lightly across his cheek. "I see the anger inside you, and the urge to destroy. But that's only half of your heritage. You need love and kindness, too."

He laughed sourly. "You don't know me."

"I do." She said it with quiet certainty. "You are a Hvee farmer, are you not? You nourish the flowers with your caring emotions. And I've seen how you are with the emp that I gave you. It's obvious that you aren't all sadism and rage. But you've never known a woman who could accept you and allow an outlet for your gentle feelings, have you?"

He was breathing heavily now, as if he wasn't sure how to cope with the emotions she was rousing. "Don't do this," he said.

She moved closer. She bent her head to his. The touch of her fingers was infinitely gentle as she circled them behind his neck. Her lips brushed his. Her slender body pressed against him. She kissed him gently, insistently. "I want you to make love to me," she whispered.

When she led him upstairs to her bedroom, he was still reluctant to surrender his self-control for fear of what he might do. She undressed him and drew him to her, but he was tense and withdrawn. She embraced him and kissed him with simple affection. This was an emotion he had learned to distrust—and yet gradually he yielded to her, because she was right: a part of him needed to love and be loved.

Their lovemaking was uncertain and a little clumsy. He was so used to a woman who needed to be taken brutally that her tenderness disoriented him. Eventually, they climaxed—at least, he did and she seemed to—and he felt tension flow out of him that he hadn't even known was there.

"Thank you," he told her sleepily, hugging her close. His body was warm, and his mind felt drugged and sated. "If I'd known, when you first came to Hvee, that it could be like this—"

"Maybe not always, for you," she said. Her voice seemed to come to him from far away. "But sometimes."

He wanted to ask her how she had known what he needed, and why she had wanted him. But he drifted into a long, deep sleep, nourished by her presence beside him.

12.

When he woke, everything had changed. Jagged rock was under his back. Glowing green lichen provided the only light. His head was pounding, and he rolled over, groaning. The walls of the cave seemed to press in on him. The air was stale, and he found it hard to breathe.

Yet, at the same time, he was sexually aroused. His pulse beat strong and hard. He clutched his crotch, not understanding why he was back here in the prison of Chthon, naked and alone.

But he was not alone. Someone was watching him. How had he not seen her before? She was standing in the entrance to the chamber where he lay. She was broad-shouldered and almost his height, with finely chiseled features and a wide, cruel mouth. Her statuesque body was draped in animal skins, and a sheathed sword hung from her belt. She stepped forward like a predator, eyeing his body. Slowly, she drew her sword.

He had no weapons. He was helpless on his back, naked at her feet.

She touched the tip of her sword to his chest, and he flinched against the cold, hard rock. He tried to cry out—but for some reason the sound was trapped in his throat. He couldn't speak.

She laughed and squatted over him, the sword still pinning him against the curve of the chamber where the floor met the wall. "I know you, Aton," she said. "Do you know me?" The tip of the blade pressed harder, breaking the skin. He felt blood starting to trickle from the wound.

He shook his head dumbly. There was a strange resonance about her, as if he had known her in some other lifetime or another universe. But if he had once known her name, he no longer knew it now.

She turned and glanced behind her. Men were standing there in bondage, hands in shackles, ankles linked with short lengths of chain. They were gaunt and bent, and their bodies were disfigured with a terrible mosaic of bruises and lacerations. They cowered from her as she surveyed them.

She turned back to Aton, loosened the skins that clothed her, and shrugged them off. Her body looked strong but trim, and the dim green light softened its curves. "Do you find me desirable, Aton?"

Again he tried to speak, but still he could not.

She grabbed his genitals in her free hand. "I asked a question. You'll answer it."

His chest ached with the need to cry out. He clenched his fists and arched his back. He parted his lips, but no sound escaped.

"Answer!" Her grip tightened, causing him intense pain. He shuddered and gasped.

She dug in her fingernails. Her eyes widened as she stared at him. He saw the eager lust in her face. He trembled with fear, but still he couldn't speak.

Her face contorted in a terrible spasm of cruelty. She twisted her wrist, then gave a savage pull. His genitals came away in her hand, spraying blood.

The spell was broken. He screamed.

13.

"What is it? What's wrong?"

Alix's arms were holding him. He opened his eyes and saw her face. He flinched from her, then saw the bed he was sitting in, the bedroom furniture, morning sunlight playing on the curtains at the window. He gasped and fell back on the mattress. His pulse was thudding. His skin was filmed with sweat.

"A dream?" she asked.

He nodded. He swallowed hard.

"Does this happen often?"

He managed to calm himself enough to speak. "I started having them recently."

"What about?" Her brown eyes were watching him with gentle concern.

He shook his head, not wanting to remember. "The prison world I told you about. Chthon. I'm trapped there, and—" he drew a ragged breath.

She pressed her body against him. Her soft flesh was warm and real, wiping away the images of horror. He hugged her close.

She moved on top of him and kissed him. He tried to respond, but then she reached down and touched his groin and he pulled himself away from her. "I'm sorry," he said, freeing himself. "I—can't, not right now." He rubbed his hands across his face.

"A little love might make you feel better," she said, with a wistful smile.

"It would. If I could. But—look, it must be late."

He glanced again toward the windows. "Malice will be wondering where I am. I should get back."

She looked at him doubtfully. "If that's what you want."

He looked at her body. It seemed infinitely desirable. Yet he was still haunted by his nightmare of Chthon, and his emotions were still entangled with the Minionette, and guilt and anxiety were tugging at him. "I want to stay," he said, realizing how inadequate it sounded. "But I can't. Maybe later—"

She stood up and put on a plain white satin robe. She walked to the window and pulled the drapes aside. "You're right," she said tonelessly. "It's more than an hour after sunrise. You should get back to your wife." She turned then, and walked out of the bedroom.

He dressed quickly, made his way downstairs, and found her waiting in the front hall. "You were very good to me last night," he said, taking her hand. He studied her face, trying to recapture the way she had made him feel. But his head was full of confusion.

"Are you wondering if I had ulterior motives for taking you in and helping you?" she asked him.

He looked at her blankly. "Did you?"

She smiled distantly. "Maybe the next time I see you I'll explain."

His face darkened. "I trusted you," he said.

She stepped away from him and opened the front door. "I know you did." She shook her head slowly. "Goodbye, Aton."

He studied her with a growing sense of suspicion. He was sure, now, that in some way she had used him. Anger and resentment surged up like an old friend, and threw a momentary fantasy into his imagination. He saw himself pushing her down onto the floor and kicking her and beating her while she sobbed and begged him to forgive her for what she had done. His pulse quickened, and he felt sick, insidious lust.

He struggled with his emotions. He could no longer tell, now, where the truth lay. In despair he turned away from her and stumbled out of her house, unable to cope with the feelings she roused.

When he had walked some distance he thought he heard her voice behind him, faintly calling him to come back to her. But by then, it was too late. He had made his decision, and he would not return.

14.

He paused at the top of the hill. The earth was soft underfoot, and the fragrance of Hvee flowers was heavy in the air. Insects buzzed around him. The trees rustled in a momentary breath of wind.

In the far distance, at the foot of the hill, he could see his home. A vehicle was pulling up in front of it. He recognized it from yesterday: it was Schenck's car. Two figures got out of it and walked to the front door of the farmhouse. They waited there a moment; then the door opened and they disappeared inside.

Aton stood with the morning sun warming his naked back. One of the people who had emerged from the car had almost certainly been Schenck. But the other? He had no idea. His intuition told him that something new was wrong; that waiting for him at the farmhouse was more bad news of some kind.

He moved reluctantly down the slope, picking his way through the field of flowers. When he reached the house, he went around to the back.

The emp was waiting for him in the yard. It jumped up and clutched at his legs. "Aton!" it squealed.

"Not now." He nudged it aside with his foot.

"Please?" It leaped onto him from behind and tried to climb his bare back. He winced as its claws scratched his skin, and it resisted when he tried to lift it off. Finally he had to pry each of its paws loose in turn. He took the little animal by its scruff and dumped it.

It chittered unhappily as it watched him walk toward the rear of the house.

He opened the back door and walked into the kitchen. Schenck was in there, sitting at the table, his bulk overflowing one of the wooden chairs. Malice was sitting opposite him. A thin, balding man was bending over her. He was in the process of locking handcuffs on her wrists. As he finished and straightened up, Aton recognized him: Strom Ten, the village law officer.

For a moment, no one said anything. The lawman pocketed his keys, looking embarrassed. Aton remained by the door, watching impassively. "What's the explanation for this?"

Schenck laughed humorlessly. "Mr. Five, surely you do not need to ask that question."

Aton eyed him, then turned back to the lawman. "Strom, what's happening?"

The lawman was a onetime Hvee farmer whose business had fallen into bankruptcy when his crops had failed. He had never wanted the job he now held, and disliked any kind of trouble. He gestured awkwardly, avoiding Aton's eyes. "Mr. Schenck has sworn out a warrant."

"What sort of warrant?" Aton's voice was still quiet, but there was tension in it, and his face was grim.

The lawman coughed. "Well—"

Schenck gestured at Malice without bothering to look at her. "This woman is from the planet Minion. I contacted the nearest Federation office overnight on my ship's transmitter. They want her shipped home."

Aton shook his head. "No. There must be some mistake."

"I already admitted everything," Malice said. "A blood sample would prove who I am. There was no point in lying."

"You see? There's no mistake." Schenck's thick lips widened in a nasty grin. His eyes were little dark slots amid the folds of flesh.

"Mr. Schenck is not only a trader, but a bounty hunter," Strom Ten explained. "You understand, Aton, if this was just up to me, it wouldn't be this way. Some of us, you know, we wondered about your wife when you first moved back here, on account of she looked so much like the woman your father brought back twenty-five years ago. But it seemed to me it wasn't our business." He saw the dangerous look in Aton's eyes and fumbled with the holster at his hip. He took out a stunner. "Now, don't go doing anything rash. Give it time, we can work through channels. Maybe we can get the Federation to grant her special status."

Schenck made a noise of disgust and lumbered to his feet. "Officer, we are wasting time. I want this woman locked in your jail, and I want an affidavit from you so I can get my reward."

"Shut up," Aton told him quietly.

Schenck grimaced. He reached in his pants and pulled out a gun of his own. It was a gas-powered projectile weapon, far more lethal than the lawman's stunner. "Farmer, do not threaten me."

Aton shook his head. "I won't let you take my wife away."

"Aton!" Malice's voice was sharp.

He looked at her. Even after the way she'd acted toward him last night, the thought of losing her seemed intolerable. He turned to the lawman. "Strom," he said, "let me just have a quiet word with you."

The officer nodded agreeably. "Well, surely. If there's anything I can do—within the law, of course—"

Aton stepped closer to the man. "Strom," he said, "I've known you since I was a boy. I'm sorry I have to do this." Unhurriedly, he seized the lawman's wrist and slammed it down onto the edge of the table.

The lawman gasped with pain. The stunner clattered to the floor.

"No!" Malice shouted.

"Stop right there," said Schenck, raising his weapon.

Aton had positioned himself with the lawman as a shield between himself and Schenck. While Strom stared

at him with hurt, frightened eyes, Aton picked him up
by his arms and threw him bodily at the bounty hunter.

The impact drove Schenck backward. The table collapsed with a crash under the weight of the two men,
and they sprawled on the floor.

Aton grabbed a kitchen knife, fell down onto
Schenck's chest, seized hold of his wrist, and stabbed
the point of the blade into the soft, chubby skin. "Let
it go!"

Schenck grunted and cursed as blood rose around
the blade. His hand trembled. Aton grabbed the gun
and wrenched it free.

The lawman had started crawling toward the stunner. Aton got there first. He grabbed the stunner,
stood up, and stepped back. "Unlock her cuffs, Strom."

The lawman gave him a plaintive look. "Aton, you
got to be reasonable. Please."

"Unlock them, or I'll stun you and do it myself."

"Officer, I'm going to report you for incompetence,"
Schenck said, holding his bleeding wrist. "I'll see you
lose your job for this."

"Damn you!" Aton aimed the stunner and discharged
it at the bounty hunter's head. Schenck grunted and
went rigid. His limbs twitched. He slumped onto the
floor, groaning.

"Aton, please!" The lawman was near panic. "You
can't do this. They'll put you away. Think of your
future, here."

Aton turned the stunner on Ten, aimed, and fired.
The lawman clutched his head in his hands, doubled
over, and collapsed on the floor.

It was suddenly quiet in the kitchen. Wood crackled
in the stove. A bird sang outside the window, and a
breeze ruffled the trees. Aton leaned against the chair
where Schenck had been sitting and looked at the two
unconscious men at his feet. The stun charge had been
set to maximum; they'd be out for at least six hours.

"Very good," said Malice. Her green eyes regarded
him challengingly. "You've taken a bad situation and

made. it infinitely worse." Her jaw had the tilt of defiance that he knew so well.

Angrily, Aton kicked the broken table. Boards splintered and fell on the floor. "First my father, then what you said to me last night, and now this. I couldn't stand it."

"If we stay here now, both of us will go to jail," she pointed out. "Assault of a law officer, resisting arrest—and I expect Schenck can come up with some other complaints as well."

He looked at her, trying to read her expression. Was she less hostile than before? Maybe last night had just been an aberration caused by the trauma of Aurelius's death. Maybe she wasn't really pregnant—or thought she was, but could still be wrong. Maybe—

He shook his head as if he could somehow get rid of the nervous thoughts chattering at him. He felt trapped. If he could only get away—

He turned suddenly. "Wait a minute. Schenck's from offworld—he has a ship here. He said it was on the landing field just outside the village."

"Are you suggesting we steal it?"

"Borrow it. If your identity is on file with the Federation, we can't use the regular transports to get offworld." Aton went and kneeled beside the man and started going through his pockets. He pulled out a sheaf of keycards. "Look at this. One to the car, one to the ship—"

"All right," Malice said, thoughtfully now. "So we get away. Then what?"

"I'll contact the Federation people at Luna. They still owe me a favor, and they'll have the authority to fix this."

She smiled at him, and for a moment he saw in her face the knowing, seductive look of the woman who had lured him to the forest glade when he had been seven years old. "You're thinking that if we go someplace new, and we start over, things will be the way they always used to be between us."

Her ability to see into him was unbearable. He reached out for her.

She pulled back and shook her head. "No."

The prohibition just made it worse. "Why not?" he demanded. He felt anguish—and anger. He saw himself seizing her, shaking her, taking her violently—

She must have sensed his turmoil, yet she seemed unmoved by it. "If we're going to do what you suggest," she told him, "we have to do it now." She held up her wrists. "Officer Ten has the key to these."

She had become a stranger to him. He tried to put aside his anger and confusion. He went over to the law officer and searched his pockets till he found a bunch of old-fashioned metal keys. It only took a moment to free Malice.

She stood quickly. "Give me that." She gestured to Schenck's gun.

"Why?"

"I don't trust your mood. You could lose your temper and kill someone."

"I suppose you could be right." Reluctantly, he handed it over.

"Shall we go?"

He looked around at the kitchen, so comfortable and reassuringly familiar. The clock on the mantel shelf, the neat row of saucepans, the old cupboard full of handmade pottery, the polished stone floor. He had grown up here. This was his home.

He turned and walked toward the door. "I need something to wear. Just a few things. I'll be right back." He walked out of the kitchen and ran upstairs.

He stripped off his pants, pulled on some other clothes, donned his sandals, and threw some items into a canvas bag. Malice remained downstairs; apparently, there was nothing she wanted.

Aton pushed the stunner into his back pocket. He walked out of the bedroom, then hesitated outside Aurelius's door. He touched the brass handle—but couldn't bring himself to go in there and look at the remains of the old man in the light of day. "Goodbye, Father," he muttered, then turned and ran down the stairs.

His eyes were sad as he walked out of the house with Malice. He stared for a moment at the lush fields of blossoms. "Never did bring the harvest in."

"So now the flowers will die." Her voice was flat and uninterested.

"You gave me a Hvee flower once. When I was too young to understand, and too young to protect myself."

She slid into Schenck's car. "That's right. I'm glad you still remember."

Aton slung his bag into the back and got into the driver's seat. He reached to pull the door shut—then heard small feet scuffing the dirt and saw the emp running toward him.

Malice saw it too. "No," she said sharply.

But the little flat, furry creature had already leaped up onto Aton's lap. It dragged itself quickly up to his chest and looked from her to Aton. "Yes?" it said. "Yes?"

"It'll starve if I leave it behind," he said.

Malice paused for a moment. Abruptly, she shrugged. She turned and looked out the window.

Aton pushed the emp up behind his shoulders and used Schenck's keycard to start the car. It rose slowly as the fans built up pressure, then glided forward along the track.

Behind them, the house receded among the lush fields of green.

15.

The dirt road followed the contours of the land. Here and there, old farmhouses and barns stood amid the hillsides carpeted in blossoms.

The road dipped through a small forest, and sunlight dimmed as tree branches closed overhead. Small animals like large rabbits with thick, stumpy legs ran for cover from the oncoming vehicle, making little bleating noises as they dived into the undergrowth.

The car reemerged into sunlight, and the village came into view at the bottom of a narrow valley directly ahead. The spire of Schenck's ship gleamed silver a little way beyond it. The houses of the village looked tiny by comparison.

"I hope Schenck traveled alone," said Aton.

"He didn't mention anyone else," Malice answered. "But even so, his ship may be fitted with an expert system to guard against unauthorized access."

Aton reduced speed as he reached the main village street. Unfortunately, this was the only way through to the landing field. Hrules tethered outside the general store turned and eyed the car as it passed. A couple of citizens stopped and stared. One of them pointed and shouted something.

"Schenck or the law officer may have told people the news about you," Aton said. "Gossip travels fast."

Malice looked back. "One of those men is getting on his hrule. I think he's coming after us."

Aton shook his head. "Too slow." He swerved around market stalls. Other villagers here were turn-

ing and staring. Several seemed to recognize the
vehicle.

"Just a couple of minutes now." He accelerated.
The little buildings passed quickly by, and the village
fell behind. Ahead was another stretch of dirt road. A
little farther, on the left-hand side, was the landing
field.

Aton took the car off the road, through a gateway,
and up a grassy slope. Years ago, this area had been
paved with hand-laid brick. Weeds had long since
sprouted in the cracks. The car wafted them aside as it
sped toward the ship, its fans whining.

Aton reversed thrust, turned the car, and cut the
power. He grabbed the emp, threw open the door,
and jumped down to the ground as the car settled
slowly on its air cushion.

"I can hear people shouting," said Malice, glancing
back toward the village. "I think they're coming after
us."

Aton tried the first of Schenck's cards in the ship's
key reader. "Invalid code," said a synthetic voice.

"Wrong way," said Malice. "Let me." She took it
from him.

The distant shouts were coming closer. "Quickly,"
he said.

There was a click and the hatch started slowly sliding sideways in its track. Immediately inside was a
steep flight of metal stairs. "You're the pilot," said
Aton. "Go on up."

She ran up the stairs. He stopped inside the hatch
and searched for the control panel. The villagers, meanwhile, had reached the landing field and were running
toward him. Some were waving farm implements. A
couple had stunners. "Stop thief!" one of them shouted.

Aton found the Close button and pressed it. Slowly,
the hatch started edging shut. The emp was still clinging to Aton's shoulders. It whimpered anxiously.

Only three inches were left between the hatch and
its frame when the first villager ran up and hurled an

old metal hoe into the narrowing gap. It jammed the door, and the hatch motor groaned and stalled.

Aton swore. He grabbed the hoe and tried to pull it free. Other villagers came running up. Hands reached for him through the gap. Someone jabbed a scythe at him, almost slicing his arm. One of the villagers at the back of the crowd took aim with a stunner.

Aton saw what was about to happen. He ducked— too late. Pain flashed in his head. Colors faded to black. He felt his knees give way, and he fell unconscious.

16.

He woke to darkness and silence. Something seemed to be pressing down on his body, like a heavy blanket. At the same time, he felt himself falling. He cried out in fear and grabbed the sides of the bunk he was lying on. Then he realized he was weightless.

He blinked in the darkness. There was a thin, faint line of light outlining the closed door of the cabin he was in, but it wasn't enough to see by.

Cautiously, he ran his fingers across the metal wall beside the bunk. He found a button, pressed it, and a glow panel came to life. He squinted in the sudden white light. The cabin was tiny, barely large enough for one bunk, a storage closet, and a hygiene cubicle.

The thing he had felt pressing down on him was an elastic restraining web. He unclipped it and sat up.

He found the emp lying on the bunk near his feet. With sudden concern he turned the little animal over, unfolding its limp body. Its eyes were closed, but it was still breathing. Evidently it, too, had been hit by the stunner. He had no way of knowing how severely its nervous system might have been affected.

Aton refastened the webbing over the emp to safeguard it from drifting up off the bed, then swung his legs down to the floor and steadied himself against the wall. For a moment, he had to fight back nausea and vertigo. He carefully oriented himself on the door, then launched himself gently toward it and thumbed its open button. The panel slid aside and he continued out into a narrow hallway.

He guided himself with handgrips in the walls, reached the central access shaft, and kicked up it. A moment later he emerged into a small control room with a single acceleration couch. He saw Malice reclining on it, her hair tangled in the zero gravity, half covering her face. Her eyes were closed, and he realized she had fallen asleep.

She had trained and served as a captain for several years, while Aton had no pilot qualifications. Still, he knew how to read the primary data displays. Quietly, he drifted to the control panel.

The ship had already traveled several light-years from Hvee and was still accelerating in accordance with a program that had been locked into the navigation computer. He didn't recognize the destination coordinates, so he found a keypad that seemed linked with the central processing system, and tried to log on.

The sound of his fingers on the keys woke her. "It doesn't work," she said sleepily. She sat up, rubbing her eyes. "I already tried. It froze up when I couldn't give the password."

Aton turned and looked at her. Maybe it was his imagination, or maybe it was the pale artificial light in the cabin, but she looked sickly. The color was gone from her cheeks. Her skin seemed puffy and slack. He frowned, baffled by the sudden change.

"Why are you starting at me?" she said.

He shrugged uncomfortably. "No reason." He glanced again at the readouts. "How did you get us offworld without access to the central processor?"

"Manually. Not easy, but it can be done."

"And where are we going?"

"I keyed in some figures that I remembered. It's a jungle world I visited once. So far as I know, there's no human outpost. It seemed like a good place to hide." The way she spoke was disinterested, without inflection, neither friendly nor hostile.

Aton nodded. "All right." He steadied himself against the control panel. "Why is there no artificial gravity?"

"I couldn't get it to work. Maybe it's been disconnected. A man as heavy as Schenck might prefer zero-G."

"I suppose." He thought back to his last conscious moments and remembered the mob trying to reach him through the hatch. "We almost didn't make it out of there. Did you take off with the hatch still open?"

"I couldn't. There's a safety interlock. I realized something was wrong, so I went down there. I still had Schenck's gun, so I used it."

Aton looked at her sharply. "You shot some of the villagers?"

"It was the only way. After they backed off, I closed the door."

"My god." He imagined her doing it; imagined the people running in panic as their companions fell down bleeding. "Some of those people I've known since I was a boy," he said, half to himself.

"Whether you knew them or not, they were a lynch mob."

"You could have used the stunner, couldn't you?"

"It was in your pocket, and you were lying on it. There wasn't time." She shrugged irritably. "Why don't you go back to your cabin? I don't feel like arguing."

The cold, disinterested tone in her voice struck at some vulnerable part inside him. It was so contrary to all his memories of her. "You know," he said, "you sound like a stranger."

"How should I sound? Adoring? Worshipful? Submissive?" She looked at him coldly.

His emotions grabbed at him. One part of him was hurt and baffled by her sudden transformation, and felt there must be some way to please her and rekindle her love. The other part—his proud, Minion side— wanted to fight back and hurt her in retaliation for the way she was hurting him. Let her feel the pain he was feeling. Punish her, somehow, till she would submit to his will and his needs. But how could he punish someone who thrived on pain? Aton repressed his anger. He

closed his eyes and deliberately thought of Alix and
the way he had felt in the brief time of their lovemaking, less than twenty-four hours ago. He pictured her
bedroom, her warm body, her gentle caresses. He
remembered the tenderness she had coaxed into life
inside him.

"Stop it!"

He opened his eyes and saw Malice's face close to
his. She had pushed herself up off the couch. Without
warning, she drew back her arm and hit him in the
face.

Her fist caught him on the cheekbone just below his
left eye. The force of the blow knocked him backward
till he banged his head against the steel wall. He was
stunned—not from the blow she had struck, but from
the fact that she had struck it. He touched his cheek
and found blood on his fingers. He stared at her in
confusion.

She settled herself back on the acceleration couch.
"Your pain," she said softly, "is delicious." Slowly,
deliberately, she unbuttoned her shirt. She slid her
hand inside and started stroking her breasts. Some of
the color had returned to her face, and she was breathing through parted lips."I never deliberately hurt you
like that before, did I? It wasn't in my nature. But you
know, if I caused you enough pain, I think it might
actually make me come."

Aton shook his head. She sounded insane. "Why
are you *doing this?*" He started toward her.

She reached for something and pointed it at him. It
was Schenck's gun. "Don't," she warned him.

He stopped abruptly. "What?"

"Give me the stunner. Otherwise, I'll hurt you. I'll
aim for your elbow or your leg. Someplace really
painful."

For a moment he stood immobile, trying to understand. But it was too much for him to deal with. He
dropped the stunner, turned without a word, and pushed
himself to the shaft. He dived down it and drifted to

the cubicle where he had awoken. He thrust himself inside and slammed the door behind him.

The emp had regained consciousness. It made a sleepy, questioning sound.

Aton pulled himself to the bunk, removed the restraining web from the little animal, and lifted it onto his chest. He was still shaking with adrenaline. He didn't know what he was doing, and didn't know what he wanted to do.

The emp clung to him and turned its head to and fro as if afraid that it would fall. The weightlessness had disoriented it. Aton stroked its fur rhythmically, trying to calm it as he also tried to calm himself.

"Food?" it said, after a little while.

He realized that he, too, was hungry. Maybe finding food would occupy his mind. He pushed himself toward the door. A man of Schenck's size would have a well-stocked kitchen somewhere on the ship, and Aton should be able to get to it without having to face Malice.

But when he tried the door, it was locked.

Aton examined it. It fit closely in its frame. There was no way to pry or bend it open, and nothing in the cabin that could be used as a lever.

In a spasm of anger he kicked out at the door with both feet. But the panel was strong; it showed no visible dent. "Damn you!" he shouted.

There was no other way out. He turned to the storage locker and pulled its door open. Inside he found a stack of entertainment cartridges—useless without a viewer—and a couple of thin plastic blankets. Underneath them was a first-aid box.

He cracked its seal and flipped the lip open. In a compartment beneath the usual ampoules, derms, and bandages was a slim packet of survival rations. He unsealed one of the chalky, tasteless calorie-bars and gave half of it to the emp.

"Bad," the animal said, handing back its share.

"You're right," Aton agreed. "But eat it anyway."

He went to the hygiene cubicle, unfolded the wash-basin, and filled a drink-bag. He floated back and per-suaded the emp to eat some of the food by alternating chunks of it with squirts of water.

Finally he stashed the rest, stretched the webbing over himself and the emp, and lay down to wait.

17.

He waited for two days. Trapped in the tiny space, he veered between anger and despair. He was haunted by dreams and memories, tormented by claustrophobia and a sense of dread. Scenes of his childhood kept coming into his mind; then moments from the recent past. He itemized everything he had lost: his father, his freedom, his home, his land, his world, and the woman who had obsessed him ever since he was a child. He thought, then, of Alix, who had seemingly been so kind. He wondered whether she'd really had an ulterior motive, or whether he had misread her in his confusion and anxiety. He wished he had acted more calmly and rationally; yet at the same time, he didn't see how it would have ultimately made any difference.

He imagined killing himself. He imagined killing Malice. In the end, he did nothing; he lay and stared at the white metal ceiling while the emp lay beside him, watching with round, puzzled eyes.

The meager supply of food ran out on the second day, but the water supply remained uninterrupted. His intuition told him that Malice still wanted him alive, even though her motives were now a mystery. Evidently, he had never really understood her. Alternatively, she had become mentally imbalanced even by the standards of her own race. He knew so little about her and her people; it was impossible for him to tell.

Gravity returned near the end of the second day. He was flung without warning against one wall, and the emp's flat body flopped half over his face. It screeched in fear, and he dragged it down beside him. This was not gravity, he realized, but G-forces. The main drive of the ship, which affected every particle within its field and thus created a sense of weightlessness, had been shut down. Malice was maneuvering for orbital injection, in which case the trip must be almost over.

Aton grabbed hold of the bunk, hauled himself over it, and lay on it facedown, holding on to its frame. The emp followed his example: it lay on Aton's back, tightly clutching him with all six paws.

The ship lurched unpredictably as Malice jockeyed it into position using the manual controls. There was a period in which nothing seemed to happen, and then a distant roaring sound as they entered the planet's atmosphere. The ship bounced and shuddered, riding pressure waves and thermals. The main part of the descent lasted fifteen minutes, until gradually the turbulence started to subside. The last minute was smooth and almost totally silent. Systems hummed and whined somewhere deep below, and there was a last-minute correction. Finally, there was a jarring thud. The structure of the vehicle groaned as she set it down on the surface of the alien world that she had chosen as their destination.

Just a few minutes later, Aton heard a metallic click from the direction of the cabin door. He stood up cautiously, testing his legs, feeling his mass as a burden now that gravity had returned. "Stay," he told the emp, pointing to the bunk. Obediently, it huddled there, tucking its paws under its body.

Aton tried the handle. It turned freely and the door swung open. Outside, he found that the passageway was empty. Evidently the door's locking mechanism had been operated remotely from the control cabin.

He considered his options. Malice possessed the stunner and the gun, and she controlled all of the ship's system. So long as he remained in it, he was at her mercy. But if he ventured outside, he had no means of survival. The planet must have been listed in the Federation catalog of habitable worlds; otherwise it wouldn't have been assigned navigation coordinates. So it probably had breathable air and edible flora. But there would be hazards, and he would need some sort of shelter.

He saw no alternative: he would have to confront her. He walked along the corridor toward the access shaft at the end. Under gravity, he would have to climb it using recessed rungs and handholds built into its walls. This would place him in a vulnerable position if she was still in the control room above, but there was no other way to get up there.

He reached the shaft and paused, listening. The ship was completely silent. He peered upward, half expecting to see her looking down at him; but she wasn't there.

He grabbed a handhold and swung into the shaft. As he did so, he heard a sudden noise of feet on metal plate. For a moment, he couldn't figure the direction of the sound. Then, too late, he realized: she had been in the passageway behind him.

Something heavy hit him between his shoulders. Aton gasped. His feet lost their grip and he fell into the shaft, dangling from his outstretched arms.

Something sharp and hard slammed across the fingers of his right hand. The pain was excruciating. He released his grip on the handhold and pulled his arm down, searching for another rung to hang on to. Quickly, she seized his other hand and bent back his fingers. He lost his grip and fell with a startled shout.

It was a twenty-foot drop. He bounced from one side of the shaft to the other, skinning his knees and knuckles, before he landed painfully at the bottom. His ankle gave him a fierce twinge of pain. He clutched it, wincing and glanced upward. She was climbing down the shaft toward him, pointing the gun at his head.

Aton lurched onto his feet and stumbled down the stairs that led from the base of the access tube to the main hatch. If he stayed in the ship, there was no way to avoid her.

Moist, warm air wafted up toward him, and he realized that she must have already opened the hatch. Did that mean she'd planned to drive him out of the ship all along?

He reached the open exit and hesitated. The world outside looked dangerous and unknown. A huge orange sun hung low in the sky, half obscured by streamers of yellow mist. The ship had set down in a clearing where the only plants seemed to be tall brown shoots that stood like vertical wooden stakes in the bare earth. Stickplants, he thought of them.

Beyond the clearing was dense jungle. The foliage was blue and purple, and the trees were festooned with flowering vines. There was a thick, heavy smell of pollen, sap, and decaying vegetation.

"Get outside," Malice shouted at him. She was walking down the stairs toward him. "Go on. Move away from the ship."

As she came closer to him, he saw that she had changed out of all recognition. The physical deterioration that he'd noticed earlier had advanced to a frightening degree. Her skin was deathly white. Her hair, which had once been such a lustrous red, was a mess of lank, black strands that seemed pasted to her head. Her face and body were grotesquely swollen, as if she had gained fifty pounds in the past two days.

"If you don't do what I say," she snapped at him, "I'll use the gun on you right now."

He saw that she meant it, and started backing away. He moved out into the clearing, stepping between the thick brown stems rooted in the gravelly soil. "You're sick," he told her. "Malice, listen to me. You need help."

She gestured irritably. "Shut up."

"Something's affected your brain," he persisted. "A

virus, maybe the same thing that killed Aurelius. Do you understand? The ship must have a med unit. For God's sake—"

He broke off with a gasp of pain as she advanced on him and kicked him hard in the groin. He clutched himself and stumbled backward, then tripped and fell.

She stood over him, pointing the gun at his midsection. "Be quiet," she told him, "or I'll kill you."

He weighed his chances of hooking one of her legs with his foot. If he tripped her, he might have an opportunity to grab the gun out of her hand. But she was just out of his reach, and she was watching him carefully.

His other alternative was to run. The little gun couldn't be very accurate. If he dodged among the stickplants that stood four and five feet tall all across the clearing—

He shouted in sudden agony. He felt as if a sharp blade had been jammed into the back of his neck. He clutched his hand to the source of the pain. There was something there, sausage-shaped, alive, trying to squirm out of his grip.

He seized it and brought it in front of his face. It had a gray, lumpy body six inches long, like a fat, misshapen worm. One end tapered to a point. At the other end was a gaping mouth lined with teeth like little knife blades. They gleamed red with his blood.

The leechworm wriggled in his grip. It was blind and had no legs. Evidently it burrowed underground, in which case the soil where he lay must be infested with them.

He flung it away and started to scramble up onto his hands and knees.

Malice kicked him in the head. He gasped. The world seemed to turn under him, and he found himself lying on his back. Darkness hovered at the edges of his vision. His head pounded painfully.

She was holding his wrist. Dimly he realized that she was tying it to one of the stickplants rooted beside him in the earth. He tried to pull away, but he was barely conscious.

She lashed his other wrist to another of the stems, so that he was pinned on his back with his arms stretched out either side. Gradually, his vision began to clear, and the dizziness diminished, though his head still gave him a lot of pain.

"I won't bother to tie your ankles," she said. "It'll be more interesting if you can thrash around a little."

Groggily, he looked at one wrist, then the other. She'd bound them with high-tensile synthetic tape. The brown stems anchoring him were about four inches thick at the base, and seemed deeply rooted. There was no way to pull free.

He shuddered as he imagined more of the leechworms burrowing up underneath his body, eager to latch onto it and suck his blood. He closed his eyes, willing himself to keep control.

"I'll be watching you for the next couple of days," she said. "With any luck, it'll take that long."

He felt sharp, stabbing pain from his left ankle and realized that the torture was starting already. Tilting his head up as much as he could, he glimpsed another of the leechworms fastening itself to his flesh.

Aton kicked his leg, hoping to shake the thing off, but its teeth clung tenaciously. He kicked again, and this time he succeeded. The creature went spinning up into the air—then fell and landed on his chest.

He squirmed in his bonds, trying to tilt his body to roll the thing off him. It had lodged in a fold of his clothing and was hunting around blindly. He squirmed some more, shook himself, and finally the leechworm tumbled onto the ground.

It was still alive, though. He felt its warm, round body wriggling alongside his ribs, heading toward his neck. Aton lifted his shoulder and held it off the ground, giving the leechworm time to wriggle a little farther. Then he slammed his shoulder back down.

He mashed the creature into the ground. Its body

burst with a muffled pop. He felt its juices slowly seeping through his shirt, warm and wet against his body.

He closed his eyes. He shuddered. The wound in his neck still hurt, and his head pulsed painfully where she had kicked him.

When he opened his eyes again a moment later, he found Malice bending over him. She had a haunted, demented expression, and her eyes shone with a strange intensity. "That felt good." Her breasts rose and fell as she breathed deeply. She reached out and trailed her fingers through the cold sweat on his forehead. "Your pain gives me so much more pleasure," she said, "than you ever did while you were alive."

She turned away from him then, and walked back toward the ship. She paused when she reached the hatch. "One thing you should know," she called to him. "I checked the records before we landed. The original survey team counted more than a thousand parasites and predators on this planet. Most of them come out at night." She glanced at the orange sun, hanging low over the jungle. "I think it should be dark in an hour or so."

She disappeared into the ship, and the hatch slid shut behind her.

18.

Within minutes, two more of the leechworms had fastened themselves to him. One of them found a way inside his shirt and sank its teeth into his waist. He managed to roll onto it and squash it. A moment later the other burrowed out of the ground beside his head and started chewing on his scalp. He banged the side of his head on it, and his ear filled with a mixture of the creature's slimy insides and his own warm blood.

He rolled over, as much as his bonds would allow. He pulled his knees up to his chest, curled into a fetal position, and kicked out at the thick brown stickplant securing his left wrist. His first attempt missed completely; but when he tried a second time, his heels made contact and snapped the stem cleanly a few inches above the ground.

He discovered, though, that he was still as helpless as before. The tape that bound his wrist to the stem was tight, and it was stuck fast. He strained to drag it up. The tape dug deep into his flesh and refused to move.

A fluttering shape distracted his attention, descending toward him from the sky above the setting sun. At first he thought it was a bird, but as it came closer he saw that it looked more like an enormous insect. It circled him warily, and he felt the breeze as it passed above his face. It had a bulbous, hemispherical body about nine inches across, and two pairs of translucent wings, like a gigantic dragonfly. Tendrils trailed from

its belly. In the dimming light, they made it look like a
large jellyfish—a flying Portuguese man-of-war.

Another of the leechworms surfaced under him, and
he rolled over quickly, mashing it into the ground.
The flying man-of-war chose that moment to land on
the bare flesh of his arm.

It wrapped its black tendrils around his skin. He
recoiled in a spasm of loathing and tried to shake it
loose, but it held fast.

For a moment it merely clung there, beating its
wings gently as if fanning itself. Then burning pain
suddenly welled up where it clutched him. Aton felt as
if his skin were being eaten by acid—and, he realized,
that was exactly what was happening. The creature
was dissolving his flesh in order to drink his blood.

He screamed and desperately shook his arm, but
there was no way to get rid of it. And from the
direction of the jungle, he heard the sound of a new
predator approaching. Its feet moved through undergrowth, then padded softly toward him.

He turned his head, whimpering in agony as the
thing on its arm drank its fill. He saw something the
size of a small dog creeping closer. It had a scaly body
and numerous legs, like a giant centipede. Its head
terminated in a sharp, pointed snout like a foot-long
beak.

Aton shouted at it, hoping a sudden noise might
scare it away. The centibeak seemed unconcerned. It
sidled closer.

A new wave of agony came from his arm. At the
same time, another of the leechworms started drilling
into his leg. He screamed as the pain grew, hammering inside his head. Up in the ship, no doubt, Malice
was savoring it as exquisite pleasure. He imagined her
watching through a night scope, clutching herself and
climaxing while he lay here slowly dying. Shamelessly,
he wept.

There was a sound from the ship. The centibeak
heard it too, and paused warily.

Aton turned his head. The hatch was opening. Light flooded out, and something came loping toward him. It made a hopeful chittering sound.

"Emp!" Aton called. "Here! Quickly!"

The emp ran over and leaped onto him, and he felt the warmth of its flat, furry body. Two round eyes looked up at him expectantly. "Aton," it said.

"Kill it," he gasped, shaking his arm with the winged bloodsucker on it.

The emp stared at him. It was a friendly, unaggressive creature. He had never told it to attack anything in its life.

Desperately, Aton bared his teeth and made a lunging motion toward the man-of-war. "See?" he said. "Bite! Eat!"

Now the emp understood. It scampered forward, seized the bloodsucker in its front paws, and sank its teeth into the bulbous body.

There was a flurry of wings. The tendrils released their grip on Aton's arm. The man-of-war lurched up and away. Blessed relief!

The emp made a little coughing noise and spat out the chunk that it had tried to eat. "Bad!" it complained. Still, it had done its job; the creature was fluttering up into the sky.

"Hand," Aton told the emp. He nodded toward his wrist.

Obediently, the emp went to his hand and touched it with its own little paws. "Hand?"

Aton tried to think what to do. The tape was too tough for the emp to sever with its teeth. The only way to remove it was to grab the free end and unwind it. "Bite. Pull," he told it.

The emp was completely trusting. Obediently, it started gnawing at the tape. Its teeth found the loose end.

"Yes! Pull!" Aton told it.

It tugged on the tape.

"More! Yes!"

The emp always tried to please. It kept tugging. Aton gasped with pain; the adhesive seemed to be ripping his skin off. He braced himself and jerked his arm as hard as he could. Finally, his wrist came free.

"Good," he told the emp. "Very good." He rolled over and quickly unwound the tape from his other wrist.

He struggled onto his feet—and almost fainted. Where the winged thing had gripped him, his arm was covered in blood. There were painful wounds from the leechworms all up and down his back and sides. One of them was still fastened on his leg; he plucked it off and stamped on it.

He turned to run for cover—but the emp was scampering back toward the ship. Aton realized that it must have gotten lonely in the little cabin. It had gone exploring and had found the hatch, which it remembered as the way they'd entered originally. It had pressed buttons on the control panel beside the hatch till one of them worked. Now it had found Aton outside, and it was happily heading back home, expecting him to follow.

Aton swore. He ran after the emp. "Stop!" he called.

Too late. Malice was standing there, silhouetted against the yellow light spilling out. The emp went running up to her, and she casually kicked it aside. Her eyes were watching Aton. She was holding Schenck's gun.

Aton turned to the emp. "Eat! Bite!" he shouted. He pointed at her.

The emp hesitated. It had never turned against a human being. Yet it was totally loyal to Aton, and he had praised it a moment ago when it had obeyed the same command.

It launched itself toward Malice, grabbed her leg, and bit.

Momentarily, she was distracted. She swore and tried to shake it off. Aton ran forwad and smashed his fist into her throat.

She fell back making choking noises. Aton's momentum carried him on top of her. They landed together inside the hatch at the bottom of the stairs.

He started prying at her hand holding the gun, but he was still dizzy, and she fought fiercely. Also, even now, the part of him that cared for her wanted to avoid injuring her. He hesitated—and she seized on his indecision. She brought her knee up and kicked at him. He lost his grip. She raised the gun and took aim.

He grabbed her wrist and wrenched it aside. The first shot went out through the open hatch, into the gathering darkness. The second ricocheted inside the stairwell of the ship. The third hit her in the face at close range.

Blood poured out of the enormous wound and splashed over Aton's forehead. He backed away, horrified.

Somehow she was still alive. She made a guttural sound, lurched to her feet, and tottered, clutching her hands to the cavity that the bullet had opened in the center of her face.

The bleeding suddenly stopped. The wound seemed to seal itself. But her face had become plastic, like melting wax. Her body, too, was changing. Her legs diminished under her until they were lumpy little stumps. Her fingers retracted, then her arms. She became an amorphous white blob, oozing out from her clothes and absorbing them.

The blob gradually changed color, darkening from white to black. It became a sludgy puddle, and started flowing up the stairs into the ship.

Aton stood there clutching his head in his hands, trying to come to terms with what he had just seen. Finally he started forward to pick up the gun where it lay on the floor just inside the hatch.

There was a muted whine of motors, and the hatch closed in front of him, almost catching his arm. He pulled back reflexively. He heard the ship's main systems coming to life. Its grav-drive started humming, and the hairs rose on Aton's arms as an intense field of static electricity surrounded the metal hull. Inch by inch, the ship started rising into the air.

Then the main power cut in and he watched in dismay as the ship lifted smoothly, like an elevator, up and out of his reach. It gained altitude and briefly gleamed bright yellow against the dark purple sky, as it entered the last rays of the setting sun.

It diminished to a pinpoint; and then it was gone.

19.

At first, he considered giving up the struggle. This uninhabited, hostile world would surely kill him no matter how determined he was to survive. Why fight against impossible odds?

But the thought angered him. Events of the past two days had structured themselves in a way that could not have been accidental. There had been a pattern in what had happened, and that meant that someone or something had planned it, and had chosen this world as the place for him to die a slow death. Very well; so be it. He would do everything he could to deprive him, her, or it of the satisfaction of seeing the plan succeed. And more: if he did somehow manage to survive, he vowed he would make his tormentor pay dearly.

He surveyed the clearing, and the jungle around it. Many of the stickplants lay crushed and broken where the ship had rested among them. He picked up one of the tough, hard plants and weighed it in his palm. Stone-age man had survived with nothing better than a crude club with which to defend himself from predators. Aton would have to do the same.

The emp came over and touched his leg. It looked up at him hopefully. "Hug?"

Grimly, Aton lifted the emp onto his back. Its companionship could be valuable to him in the hours and days to come. And the little animal could be useful to him, too. It had already saved his life; it might do so again.

Aton paused and listened. There had been a noise from the direction of the jungle. The sky was still red where the sun had set, and a small yellow moon shone overhead, shedding just enough light to see by. Peering into the dimness, he saw that the centibeak was still watching him, biding its time.

Aton crept forward. If he was to survive, it would be by thinking as a hunter, not as a victim. He hefted the four-foot stickplant, holding it like a spear, then took careful aim and flung it.

The centibeak skittered to one side, and the improvised spear landed harmlessly on the ground. The creature seemed unable to move very fast, however. Its many legs almost seemed to slow it down. Maybe he could outrun it.

At first it seemed not to see him loping toward it. Then, suddenly, it took flight. It ran in a panicky zigzag pattern across the clearing.

Aton reached the stickplant he had thrown, grabbed it, and continued chasing after the centibeak. He caught up with it just before it had a chance to plunge into a dense thicket of vegetation at the edge of the clearing. He swung the stickplant savagely, and it crunched into the creature's head.

The thing flopped onto its side. Its legs waved feebly. Aton hit it again, and it made a croaking sound and went limp.

Gingerly, he picked up the corpse by its stumpy, segmented tail. It was about as big as a fox. He lifted it in both hands, carried it to the center of the clearing, raised its body, and slammed it down onto the spiky tip of one of the stickplants that was still rooted in the ground. Then he dug his fingers into the flesh of the creature where it had been impaled and ripped it open.

"Eat," he said to the emp.

"Food?" It sounded puzzled.

Aton picked the emp off his shoulders and held it so that its face was almost touching the dead animal.

Blood was oozing and dripping. "Drink," Aton said. He trusted its instincts more than his own.

The emp licked the centibeak's blood tentatively. It turned its big eyes toward Aton. "Good!"

Aton repressed his own revulsion and joined the feast. He could not afford to be squeamish if he intended to survive. He dragged the creature's entrails out of its body and threw them aside, then drank the rest of its blood and gnawed some of its flesh from the inside of its leathery skin. It was tough and salty and pungent, but it was edible.

Any planet that had been registered by the Federation's survey corps was almost certain to have carbon-based life forms and a breathable atmosphere. Its wildlife might be hostile, but it would not be totally alien.

Aton heard a rustle of wings, looked up quickly, and saw two more of the flying men-of-war circling around him. He seized his stickplant and waited without moving as they came closer. They were blind, he realized; they must be homing in on him by sensing his body heat. He waited till they were just a few feet above, with their tendrils almost touching him, then swung his club. He hit one, then the other. They fluttered to the ground, and he stomped them quickly and methodically.

The emp hadn't liked the taste of the one that had been fastened to his arm earlier, so he didn't even bother to inspect the corpses. He was thinking ahead now, and realizing that there'd be little chance of sleep tonight. Malice had implied that many of the planet's predators were nocturnal. He'd have to remain alert to defend himself—and he couldn't even risk resting on the ground in case more of the leechworms burrowed up and fastened themselves to him. Nor did he like the idea of venturing into the jungle; there was no way to tell what carnivorous creatures and poisonous plants might be lurking in the deep shadows.

Aton went back to the centibeak, ate as much more

as he could, then left the rest to the emp. He went to
the area where the ship had set down, gathered more
of the broken stickplants, then located the entrails of
the centibeak where he had tossed them aside. A
couple of the leechworms were already chewing the
fresh meat. Aton squashed them under his heel, un-
tangled the intestines, and bit them into three-foot
lengths.

Using the entrails as rope, he lashed together
several of the broken stickplants, building a four-legged
framework that stood a few feet off the ground. He
laid more of the stickplants across it, then hoisted
himself up onto it. It creaked ominously, but it took
his weight. He would be safe from the leechworms on
this improvised platform, and it would give him a
better vantage point.

He called softly to the emp, and it climbed up
beside him. "Cold," it complained.

"Me too," he agreed. He spread its warm body
across his chest, like a blanket. He settled down, then,
for the long vigil that lay ahead.

It turned out to be less arduous than he had feared.
Early in the night, swarms of biting flies descended on
him, and he had to make a quick foray to the edge of
the jungle, where large leafy plants grew in profusion.
He used some of their leaves to wrap his feet and
arms, and he squeezed their sap over his face. It
congealed into a thick, sticky layer that seemed to
defeat the insects. He wiped some on the emp's face,
too, though it seemed less vulnerable than he was.

As the night wore on, more of the flying men-of-war
came to visit. He whacked them with the longest of his
stickplants, and the clearing was soon littered with
their corpses. Small ratlike creatures ventured cautiously out of the jungle to feed on them; and then
they, in turn, scuttled for cover when a larger animal
came prowling out of the undergrowth. It chased them
back into the vegetation, and the clearing became
quiet.

A few hours later, his skin prickled and he felt as if a much more formidable alien life form was watching him. He saw nothing, and he heard nothing; but for a moment he sensed the thoughts of another mind touching his—an intelligence that was wise and benign, and had evolved high above the simpleminded flesh-eaters and blood-suckers that Aton had encountered so far.

But the sense of contact was fleeting, and Aton was left staring into the darkness, wondering if what he had sensed was real, or if it had been an hallucination.

20.

When the sky finally brightened with the first light of dawn, he was stiff, cold, and hungry, but he was still alive. He jumped down from the platform he had built and lifted the emp to its usual position across his shoulders. Taking hold of the stickplant that he had used to defend himself during the night, he started purposefully toward the jungle. His plan was simple enough: he had to explore the surrounding territory. He needed water, and he needed food.

The trees were alive with birdsong, although not the mellow, melodic cadences he knew from Hvee. Here, it was a cacophony of raucous shrieks. He peered up into the higher branches and saw a profusion of bizarre winged things, many of them with leathery skins, like bats. Some seemed to be carnivorous; their open mouths showed pointed teeth. Others looked part insect, part reptile, with scaly skins, antennae, and bulging compound eyes.

At ground level the way forward was almost impenetrable. There were dense purple bushes whose branches were curled and tangled like tumbleweed, armored with scarlet thorns. There were mossy structures that looked like green coral but were springy to the touch. Flowering vines dangled all around, and giant insects buzzed from one blossom to the next. The jungle was formidable; but the challenge merely firmed his resolve.

Aton beat his way forward. Birds and other flying things fled from the noise he made, screaming in alarm.

Something scuttled away through the undergrowth at his feet, too quickly for him to see it or kill it.

He paused. Already, the coldness of the night was giving way to humid heat. The sap he had squeezed over his face was hot and itchy.

He glanced around at the wall of purple vegetation, then pressed onward. He had gone about twenty feet when the plants and trees abruptly gave way to an open space in front of him.

He found himself standing in a narrow path that cut through the jungle. The vines had been ripped away and the underbrush had been cleared so that bare earth was visible between small clumps of weeds. Aton wondered what sort of animal could have created such a seemingly well-used track. Or could Malice have been lying when she told him that the planet had never been colonized?

His thoughts were interrupted when he felt the weight of the emp leave his back. He turned quickly, alert for danger. Something that looked like a thick yellow vine had wrapped itself around the little animal's neck and was lifting it into the air. The emp made muffled squealing noises and waved its little paws helplessly.

The vine coiled itself like a retracting spring. It wasn't a vine at all. A fat green pod, like an enormous unripened tomato, was sitting on an overhanging tree limb. The vine was its retractable tail. On the underside of the pod, where the tail sprouted out of its body, there was a puckered opening like an anus lined with small, sharp teeth.

The tomato-pod was only ten feet above Aton's head. As the squealing emp was raised upward, he took careful aim, knowing there wouldn't be time for a second chance. He hurled his stickplant. Its pointed tip plunged deep into the creature's puckered anus-mouth.

The tomato-pod twitched and shivered. It seemed to be trying to spit out the stickplant. Green gooey stuff started oozing out and dripping down. The coiled tail thrashed to and fro, yanking the unfortunate emp from side to side. Then the tail stiffened and straightened in a death spasm, flicking the emp out of its grasp.

The emp spread its flat body and glided through the air, squealing in fright. It saw Aton below, wheeled toward him, and flopped down onto his shoulders.

"High. Bad," it chattered, clinging to him and trembling.

He patted it. "Okay," he told it. "It's okay."

The stickplant that had speared the tomato-pod abruptly fell down at his feet. He looked up and saw the creature shriveling as it squirted gallons more of the green gunk from its anus-mouth. Evidently, Aton had speared its vital organs.

He picked up the fallen stick. It was richly coated with slime. Well, if the tomato-pod had considered the emp good to eat, maybe the reverse could also be true. "Food," he said, and held the stick out.

The emp sniffed the slime and promptly started licking it, making little appreciative noises.

Aton bent down and used his cupped hands to scoop more of it off the ground. He found that it was sweet, like honey, but with a nasty bitter aftertaste. Caution told him to eat only a small quantity, and then wait; but hunger overcame caution. He devoured several handfuls. Soon he felt warmth gradually spreading from his belly, and new energy in his tired limbs.

When he and the emp were sated, he started along the path. The sun was higher in the sky now, and swarms of insects hung in the air. Aton pasted mud over his exposed skin to keep them from feasting on him and fashioned a hat from leaves to protect himself from the heat.

He walked for a while, scanning the foliage on either side of the path. Many small creatures ran from him; none approached or attacked. The jungle foliage shimmered in the air. Sweat ran down his back, where

the emp was clinging to him, and his tongue became
dry in his mouth.

"Drink," said the emp.

"I know," Aton told it. "I know."

He came to a tree whose branches were covered in
green growths hanging like elongated apples. The lowest of them was just out of his reach, so he grasped the
emp and lifted it above his head. "Pull," he told it.

It seemed to understand what he meant, and seized
the fruit in its front paws. It tugged—then recoiled
with a yelp of fear. The apple seemed to come alive.
Legs sprouted; wings unfurled. It was some sort of
insect, like a huge fly. Its thorax was the green thing
that Aton had mistaken for a fruit. It had been curled
up inside it like a snail in its shell.

The snailfly released itself from the tree and beat its
wings furiously, circling the emp. The insect's legs
seemed to end in tiny claws. They grabbed the emp,
easily penetrating its furry pelt.

The emp screamed as the snailfly sank its proboscis
into the little animal's neck. The emp leaped off Aton's
shoulders and started running wildly along the path,
trying to shake the parasite off. Aton swore and went
after them. "Emp, stop!" he shouted.

The emp screamed again and fell down on the
ground. Aton caught up and grabbed the insect in his
bare hands. Its body was covered in stiff, slimy black
hairs; holding it was like clutching a wet hairbrush. It
twisted in his grip and its proboscis came out of the
emp's neck, dripping blood.

In a spasm of fury and disgust, Aton seized the
insect's head and twisted. Its eyes burst warm and
sticky in his grip. The wings fluttered wildly. He pulled
the thing apart and threw it aside.

A great chorus of buzzing came from behind him.
He looked around and saw the whole tree coming
alive. Either the other insects had sensed the death of
the one that Aton had killed, or they had been roused
by its being plucked from the tree. The green growths

sprouted wings, dropped from the tree, and took flight,
swarming toward him.

He scooped up the emp in his arms. Its eyes were
closed and its body was limp. A large swelling had
already formed where the insect had feasted on it.

Aton ran. The sun beat down on him and his body
was soaked in sweat. Behind him, the furious buzzing
grew closer.

There was a pool of mud beside the path. Its surface
was slick and black, dotted with clumps of grass.

Aton jumped. He splashed on his back in the mud.
It was cool and wet, but not as thick as he had expected. It sucked him down like quicksand. The insects closed in overhead, blotting out the sky. He
shifted his grip so that his hand clutched the emp by its
face, covering its mouth and nose. He dunked the
unconscious creature, then joined it beneath the surface. He felt himself bump down onto the gravelly
bottom of the mud pool and forced himself to lie there
totally submerged, while his lungs cried out for air.

He stayed under till he felt himself growing dizzy
and the unconscious emp started to twitch in his grip.
Then he levered himself up till his face broke the
surface.

The insects were still there. A couple of them landed
on him, but his coating of mud seemed to offer some
protection from them. He took great gulps of air and
prepared to submerge himself again—then noticed
something new. A huge gossamer bird was floating
down out of the sky. Its wings rippled and caught
rainbows; they looked like spiderweb that had been
woven into sheets twenty feet across. Its body was a
thin tube terminating in a small spherical head with a
long, slender beak.

The bird settled like a leaf. The insects saw it—too
late. Its wings enclosed them like a shroud.

Within moments, most of the insects were stuck fast
to the spiderbird's wings, and the rest were fleeing. It
gathered its wings around itself and touched down on

the path beside the swamp. Calmly and methodically, it used its beak like a giant pair of tweezers to pick off the trapped insects one by one. It cracked them open and sucked their juices before tossing the husks aside.

Now that immediate danger was gone, Aton started struggling back to the path. He watched the huge spiderbird warily, but it showed no interest in him. Clearly, snailflies were the only food it cared for.

The emp was stirring feebly in Aton's arms. Its fur was still covered in thick mud. He wiped the sticky stuff out of the little animal's face and eyes, and it whimpered softly.

He rested a moment when he reached the path. He saw his stickplant lying where he had dropped it a few moments earlier and picked it up. He leaned on it, feeling exhausted.

But his self-pity turned quickly to anger. The hope-lessness of his situation once again roused his spirit of rebellion. If this planet was going to kill him in accordance with a plan laid down by the person or entity that had arranged for him to be stranded here, he would not surrender gracefully.

21.

He continued along the track more cautiously than before. His coating of mud quickly dried in the sun and started to crack and drop off. He managed to pull some of it off the emp, also; but the little animal remained limp and unconscious, breathing feebly.

After an hour he heard a trickling sound that seemed to come from the undergrowth at the side of the path. He paused and listened intently. By now he was dizzy with thirst and his sweat had become a thick, gummy residue. Tentatively, he stepped into the tangle of bushes and vines. The ground was firm underfoot, and he saw nothing that seemed to offer any danger. He took another step and found rocks under the carpet of vegetation. Flowing among the rocks was a small stream.

He stooped, cupped his hands in the water, and splashed it over himself and the emp, cooling his skin and washing away the mud. Then, cautiously, he took a sip. It tasted of minerals and weeds, but it seemed drinkable. He swallowed it in thankful gulps.

The emp's body was hot to the touch. Aton gently laid it in the stream, hoping to reduce its fever and revive it. He sat on a rock, tempted to drink more, but aware of the unpleasant consequences if he did. Already, he felt an urge to vomit. As he sat and waited patiently, the cramps began—merely as aftereffects of his chronic thirst. He doubled over, clutching his stomach and grunting with the pain.

It took fifteen minutes for the cramps to subside. Only then did he allow himself to take more of the water.

The emp made a coughing noise. It sat up in the stream and wiped its eyes. "Cold," it complained in a weak voice.

Aton bent and lifted it into his arms. He brushed water off its fur.

The emp blinked. "Sleepy."

"Your turn to drink." He lowered the emp to the stream. Moving sluggishly, it bent its head and lapped the water.

They rested together for a while. The emp seemed to regain its strength bit by bit, and the swelling in its neck started to diminish. Aton, meanwhile, was trying to plan ahead. If he could follow the stream, it should lead to a pool or a river. That, in turn, would attract wildlife. He could make a bow and arrow and build a refuge. If he built it well, it should be proof against most of the small parasites and predators he had encountered so far. He would recover more of his strength—

His thoughts broke off as he heard footsteps. Something was coming along the path, screened from him by the foliage. By the sound of it, it was a creature far larger than anything he had seen so far.

"Quiet," he whispered to the emp. He hunkered down among the rocks and waited, listening.

Less than a minute later he saw the animal. It was the size of a bear and was carrying a large gray sack strapped to a leather harness on its back. It had massively muscled legs terminating in huge serrated claws. Its hide was pure black, leathery, and hairless. Its heavy, tapering tail waved slowly from side to side as it walked; from the tip of the tail sprouted wicked spines like dagger blades. There was a horny carapace around its neck, and its head was like that of a wolf but twice as large, with protruding, interlocking teeth. It was a grotesque combination of saurian and mammal, and it seemed to have evolved for one purpose only: to slash, rip, and kill.

Aton remained motionless, praying silently for the beast to pass by.

It reached a point opposite his hiding place, ambled onward a couple more paces, then paused and raised its head, sniffing the air. Tentatively, then, it took a step toward Aton. Its feet crushed the undergrowth.

"Stay!" the voice came from back along the track. Aton heard more footsteps approaching—footsteps of a man.

The big black beast turned and eyed the figure striding toward it. He was heavily muscled and deeply tanned, clad in a patchwork of animal skins and hand-woven cloth. A sword hung sheathed at his hip, and he carried a heavy wooden club inset with sharp flints that gleamed in the sun. His hair and beard had been roughly trimmed within an inch of his head and face. He had the mean, feral eyes of a barbarian.

The beast growled again and turned its head back toward Aton's hiding place. Once again it took a step into the jungle.

The man came up and slammed his fist into the animal's hide. It was a blow that looked powerful enough to kill, but the big animal seemed only dimly aware of it. "Ho, dorg," he shouted. "Stay."

The animal paused. The hunter drew his sword. He parted the screen of leaves with its blade and peered into the tangle of vegetation.

"Wait," Aton whispered to the emp. Then, boldly, he stood up. He was going to be discovered anyway; it would be best to behave as if he had no reason to hide.

The black beast saw him and let out a terrible roar. Its master gave the animal another savage blow with his fist. "Stay!" he shouted again. Then he turned back toward Aton. "Show yourself. Come on."

Aton stepped cautiously forward. Taking care to make no sudden movements, he emerged into the sunlight. The yellow eyes of the black beast watched him intently, and again it growled, spraying spittle onto the soil at its feet. It lashed its tail, and the protruding blades scythed the grass.

"Who are you?" the man demanded, hefting his sword. He squinted at Aton suspiciously. His face was horribly scarred and disfigured, as if he had survived some terrible accident in which the flesh had been both ripped and burned. He wore a pack on his back and shiny white bones on a thong around his neck.

"I was abandoned on this planet," Aton said, staring straight into the warrior's hostile eyes. "I've been trying to survive."

The man eyed Aton's mud-streaked skin spotted with wounds and insect bites. He grinned and weighed his sword in his hand. "Abandoned? By who?"

"An—enemy of mine left me here to die."

The man squinted at him. He shook his head slowly. With his free hand he opened a pouch at his hip and pulled out a coil of rope woven from some kind of fibrous vine. "Turn around," he said. "Put your wrists behind you."

Aton paused. His muscles tightened. "No," he said.

The man gave a short, sharp laugh. "You do what I say, meat. Else I kill you now. Maybe slow, to make it interesting."

Aton shook his head. "I'll come with you of my free will. But I won't surrender."

The warrior stared at him. "Meat, I say one word to my dorg here, and you're dead."

"I understand that you can kill me," said Aton. Deliberately, he avoided looking at the dorg. "But if you want me alive, as your prisoner, that may be a little more difficult."

"What is it, you want a fight?" The warrior sounded incredulous.

"If it's a fair one," said Aton.

"Fair?" The man laughed. He turned to the fearsome creature beside him. "Down," he shouted at it, and pointed to the ground. Grudgingly, the beast slumped onto its belly. "Stay," he shouted again, and thumped its shoulder.

He turned back to Aton, sheathed his sword, and laid it carefully on the ground. He shrugged off his backpack, but kept hold of his club. "This fair enough for you?"

"I have no weapon," Aton pointed out.

"That's your problem, meat." Suddenly, savagely, the warrior swung his club toward Aton's stomach.

Aton leaped backward. He was just fast enough to evade the blow, but he lost his balance, flailed his arms, and fell.

The warrior closed on him and aimed a kick at his head. Aton dodged, rolled aside, seized the man's ankle, and tried to topple him.

The warrior swung his club again. It hit Aton's arm, and the pain was instant and paralyzing. He gasped, clutching his elbow.

The warrior dropped his club, fell onto Aton's chest, and grabbed him by the throat. He squeezed hard.

Aton flailed helplessly. He tried to pry the man's hands away, but his adversary was too strong. He tried to pull up his knees to kick the warrior off him, but the man foresaw that and shifted quickly, evading the move. Still he kept his grip on Aton's throat.

Aton felt himself starting to black out. The warrior's face was just inches away, leering down. The man was panting, and his eyes were wide. His skin was flushed as if the violence was arousing him sexually.

In desperation, Aton brought his head up and seized the warrior's nose in his teeth. He bit with all his strength and hung on. Blood ran out over his face.

The warrior let out a roar of pain and rage. His grip relaxed. Aton drew on his last remaining strength, reared up, and threw the man off. He groped around, dizzy from lack of oxygen, and seized the warrior's club where it lay on the ground.

The warrior was stumbling backward, his face running red. He stooped, seized his sword where he had laid it aside, and drew it from its sheath. He wiped blood out of his eyes, then ran at Aton.

Aton tried to knock the blade aside, but the club was too heavy in his wounded arm. It twisted out of his grip, and once again he landed on his back. The warrior planted one booted foot on Aton's chest and pressed the tip of his sword to Aton's throat.

For a moment neither man moved. Aton lay gasping for breath, staring up into the warrior's face. The warrior glared down at him, holding his free hand to his face in an effort to staunch the bleeding. "Bastard," he swore. "Ought to kill you right now."

Aton said nothing. He waited.

The warrior scowled. "All right, turn over, meat."

Slowly, carefully, Aton did so. His arm hurt terribly; he feared the blow from the warrior's club might have broken it.

"Hands behind you. Come on!"

The point of the sword was now nudging Aton's back, between his ribs. He did as he was told.

The warrior fell down on him, grabbed his wrists, forced them together, and bound them quickly with the rough rope. Then the man drew back. "Stand up."

Aton did so. His arm sent fierce twinges of pain, but he forced himself to ignore it.

The warrior was still bleeding from his nose. He went to the dorg, opened a pouch on its harness, and pulled out a dirty rag. He tilted his head back and squeezed the rag to his face for a while. Aton lay on the ground, waiting.

Eventually the warrior stashed the bloodsoaked rag and turned to his dorg. "Up!" he shouted, kicking it in the ribs. Then he turned back to Aton. "All right, we got a mile to cover, maybe more."

"Wait," said Aton. "I have a friend."

The warrior squinted at him. "You what?"

"Emp!" Aton called.

Cautiously, the emp emerged from the undergrowth, parting the long grass and bushes with its little paws. It

saw Aton and ran to him, chittering nervously. It
clung to his chest, then looked over its shoulder at the
warrior.

"What's that?" the man demanded.

"A pet," said Aton.

"Yeah?" The warrior peered at the emp, then nodded slowly to himself. "Sure, bring it along." He shouldered his pack. "Yeah, we'll take care of it, sure
enough."

22.

The trail was littered with fragments of deadwood. The ground was stony underfoot. With his hands tied behind him and the weight of the emp on his back, Aton had difficulty keeping his balance. But the warrior showed little interest in Aton's problems. He followed close behind, cursing and smacking the backs of Aton's legs with his wooden club whenever the pace faltered.

Aton walked in silence, grimly repressing his anger. The flints embedded in the warrior's weapon jabbed his skin painfully, but he knew that if he complained, the man would merely mistreat him more. Eventually, perhaps, there would be an opportunity to equal the score; but now was not the time.

The jungle was a tangled wall of purple and green on either side of the path. Birds screeched and insects buzzed, and small things rustled through the undergrowth. For the most part, though, the presence of the warrior's fierce black dorg seemed to scare the predators and parasites away.

After they'd been walking for an hour, the trail became steep and the foliage began to thin out. Through gaps in the trees Aton glimpsed a bare hilltop where some sort of primitive fort had been built. Evidently, this was their destination.

They finally emerged from the jungle onto a wide strip of blackened earth where all the trees had been felled and all vegetation had been burned to ash. Beyond it was a trench filled with plants like giant

Venus's flytraps, their jaws gaping wide, spines dripping with poison. Beyond the trench was a stone wall, and beyond that a stockade.

The wall was still under construction. Gangs of ragged men were hauling boulders and stacking them to form a barrier twenty feet high. The men worked in grim silence, grunting and sweating under the sun. Black-uniformed guards rode among them on dorgs. screaming orders and jabbing the workers with long pointed sticks.

All of the guards appeared to be women. All of the workers were men.

The warrior nudged Aton to the edge of the trench, and the plants in it twitched and turned slowly toward him, sensing his body heat. He looked down and saw bones and scraps of partially digested flesh lodged in some of their wet, pink vegetable mouths.

"Wait there," the warrior told him. "Hey! Huro!"

The tallest of the guards turned her dorg. "That you, Baz?" She shaded her eyes. "What happened to your face?"

He rubbed some of the dry blood off his nose. "Nothing," he said. The word was a surly grunt.

"Who's that with you?"

"Garvin, in the bag here." He slapped the sack draped across the back of the dorg. "This one I found in the jungle. Says he's from offworld."

The woman turned in her saddle. "You," she shouted, pointing to the two men nearest her. "Lower the bridge."

They dropped the stones they had been carrying, ran to a wooden winch, and started turning it. A catwalk made from logs swung down and thumped into position across the trench.

"Walk," said the warrior, thwacking Aton with his club.

Aton started forward. He didn't doubt that if he refused, he would die.

The warrior and the dorg followed him across. As

soon as they reached the other side, the bridge was raised behind them.

Aton stood calmly with the emp still clinging to his back, peering nervously over his shoulder. The woman named Huro walked her dorg around him, looking him over. She had a thin, boyish body and a pale face with dark, glittering eyes. She wore her black hair in a crewcut.

She pointed to the emp and looked at Baz. "What's that on his back?"

"Some sort of animal. Maybe from offworld, like him. He says it's his pet."

Huro threw her head back and laughed. It was a sharp, ugly sound. "All right, let's take him—"

She broke off, distracted by a disturbance among the workers on the wall. One of them had collapsed. He was on his hands and knees in the dirt, gasping for breath. Sweat was dripping off his face, and he was shaking with exhaustion.

"Get up, scum!" the nearest guard screamed at him, dismounting from her dorg. She uncoiled a whip that hung at her belt, swung it in a wide arc, and brought it down savagely across the man's naked back. "If you don't work, meat, I'll kill you."

The man slumped onto his belly and moaned.

"Get up!" the guard screamed again. She started whipping him in a savage frenzy, and blood sprayed where the leather sliced his skin.

"Wait here," Huro snapped at Baz and Aton. She stepped down from her mount, walked over, and took the woman's arm, restraining her. "What's the problem? Spinks wants special treatment?"

The woman with the whip paused, breathing heavily from her exertions. "What shall we do with him, Huro? Every day, trouble. Lazy scum. Gut him? Or dump him?" She jerked her head toward the trench.

The man on the ground rolled over. "No!" he

moaned. He crawled toward Huro and clutched at her booted feet. "Please!"

"Get your hands off her." The guard raised her whip again.

"No need for that," Huro said calmly. "It looks to me as if Spinks wants a little rest. He's tired. Well, I can understand that." She gave him a cruel smile.

Spinks clutched his face between his hands. "Huro, please!"

Huro raised a whistle that hung on a chain around her neck and blew three short blasts. The rest of the men stopped what they were doing, set down their burdens, and turned toward her.

"You four." Huro pointed to a group standing at the bottom of a flight of big stone stairs that led to the top of the wall. "Pull that slab out a couple of feet." She pointed to a big rock at the base of the stairs.

They went to it, bent down, and heaved at it, grunting and straining. Gradually, they edged it to one side.

"Now take Spinks here and sit him on the bottom step."

The men grabbed Spinks's limp, bleeding body, lifted him under the arms, and pulled him back. "Please," he kept moaning. "Please!"

"It's *all right,* Spinks," Huro assured him. "You're going to spend the rest of the day sitting down. Maybe tomorrow, as well. We'll make sure of that." She turned to the men. "Now pull that stone back."

Spinks suddenly realized what was going to happen to him. If it was dragged back to its original position, the rock would crush his legs below his knees, pinning him. "No!" he screamed.

"Hold him!" Huro snapped. Several men hurried to obey.

"No!" Spinks screamed again, trying to fight them off.

"Shut up, scum," snapped one of the men.

"It's your own fault," said another. "You should've pulled your weight."

Meanwhile, the other four were dragging the big stone back. Its surface was rough and granular. Thousands of sharp, tiny facets gleamed wickedly in the sun.

"You there," Huro turned to three others. "Help them lift it. Tilt it up and let it drop."

They did as she said. It crunched down onto Spinks' shins, splintering them. He let out a terrible scream. His fingers scrabbled desperately, hopelessly at the rock, leaving fragments of skin and blood on its rough surface. He writhed and screamed again.

Huro blew a long blast on her whistle. The work crew returned quickly to their places and picked up where they had left off. Those who were carrying boulders to the top of the wall had to walk right past Spinks, treading on the slab that pinned his legs, so that their weight mashed its jagged surface more deeply into his flesh. He wept and clutched futilely at them as they passed, but they ignored him.

Huro walked back to where Aton was waiting with Baz. She eyed Aton as if wondering how long it would take to reduce him to the same kind of mindless obedience that the rest of the men showed her. Then she gave him a twisted smile.

"Welcome to Chthon," she said.

23.

Huro rode her dorg through a gap in the stone wall. Aton and Baz followed, with Baz's dorg trailing behind. Just inside the wall was the stockade, built from tree trunks hammered into the ground. Aton was led through a gateway and found himself in a big, square compound with guard towers at each corner. Half a dozen buildings constructed from logs were ranged around a central yard of packed earth. It looked like a military parade ground.

Two more black-uniformed female guards came running over. One of them removed the heavy gray sack from the back of Baz's dorg and dumped it on the ground. She threw a rope around the animal's neck, then led it away toward a building that looked like a barn. The other woman waited for instructions.

Huro gestured at the sack on the ground. "Pick that up."

The woman stooped and pulled the sack across her shoulders. She stood up shakily, grunting with the effort. "We'll go to the guardhouse," said Huro, turning her dorg and leading the way without glancing back.

They followed her across the yard to a small cabin with barred windows. She dismounted and waited while Baz, Aton, and the woman carrying the sack walked in ahead of her.

Inside were a couple of wooden stools, a crudely made table, and a series of jail cells with thick wooden bars. The place smelled of unwashed flesh, urine, and

wet straw. A couple of the cells were occupied, but
the bars were so thick and spaced so closely that Aton
couldn't see the prisoners. An insistent moaning was
coming from a cell at the end.

"Quiet," Huro said in a conversational tone of voice.
The moaning immediately ceased.

"Dump it on the floor," she told the woman holding
the sack. "Yes, there. Good. Now go get Quentain."

The woman in black turned and ran out of the
building.

Huro pointed to the sack. "Open it," she snapped
at Baz.

He kneeled down, loosened a thong at the neck of
the sack, and rolled it back. A man was inside, naked
and smeared with blood. His body was grotesquely
swollen from insect bites, and there were ugly fester-
ing wounds on his chest and arms.

Huro kneeled down and peered at the man. "Is he
alive?"

"Yeah, just about." Baz kicked the sack, hard. The
man groaned and mumbled something, but his eyes
stayed shut.

Huro prodded the unconscious man "Quentain's
going to take care of you, Garvin," she said in the same
conversational tone. "Then, when you're feeling better, she's going to show everyone what happens to a
man who thought he could run out on us."

"You wanted to see me, Huro?" A woman was
standing in the doorway.

Huro straightened up. "Yes, Quentain. Come on
in."

The woman who walked into the fetid little room
had long wavy blond hair, a heart-shaped face, full
lips, and clear blue eyes. She could have been a glam-
our model; even without makeup, her face seemed to
glow. She wore leather sandals, a simple cotton jacket,
and pants bleached pure white. Her body looked gen-
erous and feminine under the simple clothes.

"Baz found Garvin for us," said Huro. "He needs some of your tender loving care."

She touched slender fingers to the unconscious man's face and neck. She smiled strangely, as if Garvin's condition gave her a devious kind of pleasure. She pressed one of the swellings on his chest, and it oozed pus streaked with red. She rubbed the discharge slowly between her finger and thumb.

"Can you handle it?" Huro asked.

Quentain hesitated, as if reluctant to look away from the victim in front of her. "Oh, yes." Her voice sounded lascivious. "He'll be fine." She stood up, finally, and nodded to Huro. "I'll see to that." She noticed Aton then. "Who's he?"

"Baz found him in the woods."

Quentain approached Aton and ran the palm of her hand over his shoulders and chest. She walked around him, and squeezed one of his buttocks, then his thigh, as if he were cattle up for auction.

With his wrists tied behind him, there was little that Aton could do. He watched her as she walked back in front of him. Her soft beauty was an illusion; she had a cold, sadistic detachment. She finished sizing him up and nodded to herself, satisfied.

"Shouldn't you see to Garvin here?" said Huro. There was a deferential tone in her voice. She sounded as if she was uncomfortable dealing with Quentain.

"I'll send someone to get him," said Quentain. She gave Aton another look, then tossed her long blond hair and walked out.

Huro turned to Aton and Baz. Her expression was unreadable. "All right, you two. I'd better turn you over to Oris."

24.

She led them to the only two-story building in the compound. Its lower level was built from boulders, its upper level from logs. Two huge dorgs guarded its entrance, supervised by half a dozen brawny black-uniformed women armed with swords, maces, and spears.

Two of these guards escorted Aton, Baz, and Huro through a pair of massive doors and up a narrow wooden spiral staircase. When Aton emerged at the top he found himself in a long room with a table at one end. Dim light filtered through arrow-slits at intervals around the walls, illuminating an array of torture devices.

He walked with his captors past a rack, a pillory, a whipping post, a coffin lined with spikes, and a cross. Thumbscrews, fingernail pincers, leg spreaders, hoods, castration pliers, studded paddles, lashes, and whips hung from hooks on the walls. Almost every implement was stained dark with blood. Aton assumed that they were arrayed deliberately to intimidate prisoners, but the display was effective, nonetheless.

A woman was sitting behind a table at the end of the room. Her long, straight black hair was pulled back from her face, revealing high cheekbones and a wide, proud mouth. She was heavily built and he guessed that if she stood up, she would be almost his height. Aton stopped and stared at her stupidly. He recognized her from his dream—his nightmare at Alix's

111

house, on Hvee. It was impossible; but the reality of it was before him.

"Show some respect, meat," snapped the burly guard behind him. She whacked the backs of Aton's legs with her sheathed sword, making him fall down onto his knees. Baz, he realized, had already kneeled beside him.

"Baz found Garvin and brought him in," Huro was explaining to the woman behind the table. "He found this one, too." She gestured at Aton. "Says he's an offworlder."

The woman sitting behind the table nodded. "Baz, you did well. You'll get your reward."

The warrior inclined his head. "Thank you, Oris."

"What happened to your face?"

He looked uncomfortable. He jerked his head at Aton. "He put up a fight."

"He did?" Her voice showed interest. She stood up. "You can go, Baz. And you, Huro."

Aton was aware of them leaving, but his attention was still on the woman in front of him. He felt as if reality had shifted around him—as if space had twisted, somehow.

She walked around the table and sat on the corner, looking down at him. "So, you're a fighter. Tell me your name, where you're from, and how you came to be here." Her voice sounded calm and competent, as if there was no question he would tell her whatever she wanted to know.

"Aton Five," he said. "From the planet Hvee. I was—traveling with someone who abandoned me here." He hesitated. "Is it true that this is Chthon?"

She laughed derisively. "You ask a question without my permission? Hurt him." She gave the order without bothering to look up.

One of the heavily muscled women stepped forward quickly, seized Aton by his hair, and punched him in the face. Instinctively, he tried to bring up his hands to defend himself—but they were still tied behind his

back. He lost his balance and fell on his side. The emp
squealed in fright and jumped off his back.

"What's that?" Oris asked sharply. "Vermin? Kill
it."

"No!" Aton shouted. He squirmed around and threw
himself over the emp, covering its body with his own.

The guard had raised her spear. She paused uncertainly.

Oris gestured for her to lower her weapon. She
looked at Aton curiously. "You'd sacrifice your life
for an animal?"

He lay there for a moment with his thoughts in
turmoil. He had acted out of pure instinct. Slowly, he
rolled away from the emp. "It's more than an animal.
It's intelligent and it's been my companion."

Oris walked over and looked down at the emp. She
prodded it with her toe, and it backed away, chittering
nervously. She gestured dismissively. "All right, we'll
take care of it." She turned to her guard. "Put it in
one of the empty jail cells. Feed it the same as the
prisoners get."

"No!" Aton shouted again. He tried to struggle up
onto his feet, but the guard kicked him casually aside
and grabbed hold of the emp. She bundled it under
her arm, ignoring its cries of surprise and fear, and
carried it away.

Aton turned to the woman named Oris. He was
suddenly pale with rage. "You kill that animal," he
said, finding it hard to speak through the tightness in
his chest, "and I'll kill you. I swear it."

She shook her head like a schoolteacher regretting
the stupidity of a new student. "Normally," she told
him, "I'd have you disemboweled for threatening me.
But I think we can make use of your anger and your
hate." She gestured to the guard. "Pick him up."

Strong hands lifted Aton to his feet and held him.
He stood, still glaring at Oris, and said nothing.

"There are four things that every man in this camp
understands," Oris continued, walking closer to him.
"I will tell them to you now. See that you remember

them. First, you are now my property, and you will never, ever be free." Her dark eyes stared into his. "Second, you will do exactly what I say, and what my servants say, or you will suffer the most terrible punishments that you can imagine. Third, if you obey fully, you will be fed and clothed and possibly even rewarded. Fourth, you will discover that I never lie. If I tell you something, it is so." She turned to the remaining guard. "Put him in the room downstairs. Once he's in there, you can untie and feed him."

Aton struggled and kicked, but with his arms pinned, he was helpless. The guard started hustling him out of the room.

"One other thing," Oris called as he was dragged away. "You will see your animal again, alive, so long as you do as you're told. And yes, this is an undeveloped area on the planet Chthon. We used to be convicts, condemned to the prison underground. But as you can see"—she gestured at the room and the camp beyond it—"that situation has changed."

25.

They put him in a room with log walls, a wooden ceiling, and a floor of hand-planed boards. There was a large bed with a soft straw mattress. A bowl and a pitcher of water stood in one corner. A small barred window looked out onto the open yard at the center of the compound.

The room was larger than he expected, and it was clean. Aton lay on the bed and tried to massage the stiffness out of his wrists, now that they were no longer tied behind him. Then he rested for a while with his eyes closed, trying to look inside himself for the strength that he needed.

Escape was obviously out of the question. Even if he managed to evade his captors—which seemed unlikely—there was nowhere to run to in the hostile wilderness outside, and they would track him and bring him back as easily as they had brought back Garvin.

In any case, before he could turn his back on Oris and her sadistic female guards, he needed answers to more of his questions. How had he dreamed of her face and name, days before meeting her? Was it precognition, or had someone or something planted the vision in his sleeping mind? Had she somehow played a role with Malice, abandoning him here on Chthon? That seemed unlikely; Oris had inspected him as if he were a total stranger.

But if this was the planet Chthon, what had happened to it in the past months? He remembered a world whose surface had been developed as a pleasure resort named Idyllia—a place for the rich to relax among soft meadows and open, rolling hills. The notorious prison of Chthon had been restricted to caves beneath the planet's crust.

Six months ago, the tourists had been evacuated and the plasma intelligence at the heart of Chthon had been annihilated, largely thanks to Aton's efforts. He had freed the prisoners to take over Idyllia's verdant paradise, where they could create a society of their own. That had been his grand, compassionate gesture. What had gone wrong, he couldn't imagine—assuming that Oris spoke the truth and this was, in fact, the surface of Chthon.

He sat up quickly as he heard a heavy bar being shifted outside his cell door. One of Oris's beefy female guards came in carrying a tray laden with bowls of food. A second guard stood behind her, armed and ready.

"Smells good," Aton said cautiously, as she set the tray at the end of his bed.

"Too good for you, scum."

"You mean I'm getting special treatment?"

The big woman laughed. "Later tonight, that's when you get the treatment."

"Shut it," said the one near the door. "Don't talk to the prisoner."

When Aton was alone again, he sampled the food. There was a rich meat stew, some pink root vegetables that tasted like boiled potatoes, and slices of jungle fruit. He could see no point in not eating; he would have to, sooner or later, and they could poison him then as easily as now. So he dug into the food greedily, wondering why he was being treated so well.

After the meal he tried again to relax, emptying his mind of all questions and fears. Through the window, he heard distant shouts from the guards supervising the men building the wall. A whip cracked and a man screamed.

Aton buried his head in his arms to shut out the

sounds. All too soon, he guessed, he would be out there with the rest of them. Best to rest; he would need his strength.

But why was this primitive fortress being built, and how had it come to be established in the first place?

Weariness finally slowed his thoughts, and he slept.

26.

He woke to new sounds. There were marching feet, jingling harnesses, and men shouting.

Aton stood on his bed and peered out of the window. The light in the sky had dimmed, and shadows had grown long. A band of warriors, larger and fiercer-looking than the slaves working on the wall outside, were walking into the compound through the main gate. Behind them came harnessed dorgs with bulging sacks strapped to their backs.

Oris and several of her guards were standing on a platform at one end of the yard. The warriors pulled the sacks off the backs of their dorgs and unpacked a rich assortment of dead wildlife that had been culled from the surrounding jungle. Then the men kneeled respectfully while Oris inspected their plunder.

Aton saw now where his meat stew had come from. A camp as big as this would need a regular food supply; evidently, some of the men were trusted sufficiently to be allowed out in hunting parties.

After the inspection, the dead meat was hauled away and the warriors and their dorgs disappeared in the direction of a large building that looked like a barracks.

Next, into the yard came the work gang that Aton had seen building the wall. Few of them managed to stand straight; some were so exhausted they could barely stand at all.

Their guards, mounted on dorgs, drove them into the center of the yard. A cart appeared, loaded with

bones and scraps of raw meat. The sight roused new
energy in some of the men, and they stumbled forward
with outstretched arms.

A woman climbed up to the cart and started tossing
food into the crowd. The men fought savagely, literally ripping morsels from each other's mouths. On the
platform at the end of the yard, Oris made herself
comfortable in a large chair and watched, idly chatting
to her companions. Occasionally she pointed to one
man or another, as if comparing their viciousness and
cruelty in stealing from one another.

The woman on the cart threw the last of the scraps
among the men, then turned away with no apparent
interest. Aton saw that the weakest members of the
group had been left with virtually nothing. They were
already scrawny and hollow-eyed; at this rate, they
would soon starve. This was survival of the fittest
reduced to its crudest, most brutal level.

Aton turned suddenly as he heard the door of his
room open. His jailer was bringing in a bowl of soup
that smelled rich and strong. She set it on the floor,
then turned and left without a word.

Was this some sort of a test, to see if he would
cheerfully eat the soup after watching starving men
battling for scraps of rotten meat? Aton shrugged and
picked up the bowl. The camp seemed designed so
that only the strong would survive. There was no way
he could help his fellow prisoners. This being so, it
was pointless to concern himself with their suffering.

The soup was delicious. He ate heartily.

27.

Someone was in the room with him. Hands touched his naked body, and a woman laughed softly. For a moment he thought he was back in his home on Hvee, in bed with Malice; then he remembered where he was, and felt fear.

The room was almost totally dark. Two black silhouettes were bending over him. He tried to sit up—but discovered that he had been tied to the bed. His mind felt fuzzy; he tried to think back. He'd become drowsy half an hour after eating the soup. That was the last thing he remembered. Evidently it had been drugged.

"What—" he began, peering up at the shadowy figures.

"Quiet." A hand gripped his chin, and something was pushed into his mouth. It was a wad of leather, a plug about three inches long and slightly less than two inches in diameter. Strong hands buckled a strap around behind his neck, holding it in his mouth, filling it so that he couldn't speak.

He turned his head from side to side and made angry smothered noises.

A hand grabbed his genitals. "Behave yourself!" It sounded like Oris's voice. The hand squeezed him warningly.

Aton shuddered. He remembered his dream of Oris standing over him in the caves of Chthon, ripping his genitals out of his body.

"Just be quiet," said another voice. Quentain; he

was sure it was her. "You'll feel no pain." She started rubbing perfumed oil into his body, beginning at his shoulders and working slowly downward. Her hands moved in an easy, hypnotic rhythm. A couple of times she bent close to him and he felt her nipples brush across his chest. Then she got up onto the bed and sat on his thighs, her naked buttocks like a warm, soft cushion pressing against him.

Aton was still dizzy from the drug. Even though he had no intention of cooperating with his captors, his body was beginning to respond of its own accord. Warm oil was wiped around his genitals, and knowing hands caressed him there. He felt a tension growing, and he squirmed in his bonds, angry that he couldn't resist.

"He's ready," said Quentain's voice. She traced fleeting, tantalizing patterns with her fingertips, then withdrew.

"Good." Oris swung her leg over and sank onto Aton, engulfing him. She wriggled her hips, then leaned forward, bracing herself with her hands on his chest. She moved methodically, as if to satisfy herself as efficiently as possible. Within moments, she climaxed.

Quentain took her place. She was lighter and moved on him cautiously at first, touching all around the junction between their bodies as if examining him there. Aton felt himself becoming more aroused—but she felt it too, and withdrew for a minute. Slowly, then, she leaned forward so that her bare breasts pressed against him. He groaned, tantalized by her flesh, and she grunted with satisfaction as if his torment pleased her.

Soon she, too, climaxed, and Oris returned for more. The two women used him for their pleasure for the whole of the next hour. They never allowed Aton to lose his erection, but they never allowed him any chance of orgasm, either. By the end of it his groin felt swollen, and his whole body was glowing and tingling with a need for release.

"It almost seems a pity," Quentain murmured, when they finally finished and stood over his naked body.

"No." Oris's voice was matter-of-fact. "He deserves what he gets." She walked away from his bed toward the door, and he heard a rustle of fabric as she put on her clothes. "Guard!" she called.

Aton strained helplessly in his bonds, and his rage mounted. He imagined what he would do if the positions were reversed so that Oris and Quentain were lying naked in bondage and he was standing over them, free to inflict as much pleasure or pain on them as he chose. The thought was intoxicating—which made it all the more frustrating.

The door to his room was opened by the guard. "Untie him, Oris?"

There was a moment's hesitation. "No. Some self-restraint will be good for him. Remove the gag, but leave the ropes." And she left, with Quentain following her.

The guard walked in, undid the strap behind Aton's head, and pulled the fat leather plug out of his mouth. The muscles of his jaw ached, and his lips were numb and bruised.

The guard left and locked the door, and Aton found himself lying wide awake with no way to vent his frustration. He tried to turn his thoughts away from his helplessness, back to simpler times. He thought of his childhood on Hvee—but that in turn brought back memories of Malice, and the way she had seduced and captivated him.

He twisted and tugged at the ropes holding him to the bed. Was his whole time to be spent as a victim, unable to control his life?

A strange cold prickling sensation swept over him, and he shivered. He felt as if an invisible hand had brushed across his body. He remembered when he had spent the night outside in the clearing. He had felt, then, another mind touching his. This was the same sensation, but far more intense.

"We are listening. We will try to help." The thoughts formed themselves inside his head, and he sensed a creature that was enormous and diffuse, like a galaxy of stars.

"Who are you?" he muttered, wondering if he was merely talking to a hallucination that he had created inside his own head.

"We are watching. Try to be patient."

The presence in his mind vanished as quickly as it had come, like a cat leaping away into the jungle, disappearing into the night.

28.

They came for him the next day, untied him, and dragged him naked into the yard. He blinked in bright sunlight as cool morning air raised goosebumps on his bare body. The guards handled him roughly, and no one would tell him anything. He felt a rising sense of dread.

The guards marched him to the infirmary, threw him onto a rough wooden table, and buckled heavy leather straps across his wrists, elbows, ankles, thighs, throat, chest, and abdomen. By the time they finished, he was unable to move and could barely even breathe. The guards still refused to say anything. They stamped out of the room and slammed the door behind them.

He was still able to turn his head. He looked to the left and saw a board on which had been laid out a scalpel, pliers, several rusty clamps and tweezers, needles, thread, and a wooden-handled dagger.

He shuddered and looked to the right. Three beds stood against the wall. One of them was occupied. "Garvin," Aton called, recognizing the man.

He was sitting on the bed with his eyes closed, his head resting against the wall. At the sound of his own name he half-opened his eyes and looked dully at Aton. He said nothing.

"What are they going to do to me?" Aton heard the panic in his own voice. Fear was gnawing hard at him now, and he didn't know how to control it.

"Cut you," said Garvin. Slowly, his eyes fell shut again.

"Help me! Come and undo these straps!"

Slowly, Garvin shook his head, still with his eyes closed. "Paralyzed," he said. "Quentain cut my spine."

"My god. Can't you move at all?"

Garvin shook his head again. "No." He paused. "You'll live," he said. "I won't."

"Get me free and I'll help you," said Aton.

Garvin smiled dreamily. "Only thing that'd help me, man, is if you killed me."

A door behind Aton's head creaked open and footsteps approached. Quentain's face appeared above him. She eyed him coolly. "You weren't given permission to talk."

Aton stared up at her, breathing fast, feeling his heart thudding painfully.

She picked up the dagger from the board beside him. Slowly, thoughtfully, she pressed just the tip of it into his chest. Aton flinched from the pain. "Why?" he gasped. "Why are you doing this?"

"Quiet!" She raised her hand and stabbed the blade into his shoulder, then started twisting it. Her eyes widened and her lips pulled back from her teeth as she saw his face contort with pain.

Aton struggled not to scream. His shoulder throbbed and blood started trickling down.

She withdrew the blade, then walked slowly around him, trailing her fingers across his body. She breathed deeply, and pulled her shoulders back, so that her breasts were clearly outlined under the tight white uniform. The violence against him had obviously aroused her. She kneaded his flesh with her hand, and he remembered how she had massaged him during the night before having sex with him. "I can do whatever I want to you, here," she said, trailing the tip of the blade down one of his thighs and watching intently as Aton shuddered and made little groaning noises. "You do understand that, don't you?"

"Yes," he said.

"Did I give you permission to speak?" She jammed the blade savagely into the sole of his foot. "Did I?"

He clenched his teeth against the pain. Tears sprang from the corners of his eyes. Mutely, he shook his head.

She was breathing very heavily now. She loosened the waistband of her pants, thrust her free hand inside them, and started touching herself. "Very good, Aton. You've learned something." He gave his thigh a little jab and watched his flesh quiver as he tried helplessly to pull away from her. "Fear excites me, did you know that?" She moved up alongside his face and stared down into his eyes. She held the blade where he could see it, then lowered it out of his field of vision. She lightly pricked his throat, then his sternum, still watching his face intently. She pricked his chest, his belly, then trailed the blade still lower, down across his abdomen, moving it slowly, inexorably toward his crotch.

Aton lost all self-control. "No!" he screamed.

The blade clattered harmlessly onto the table and Quentain clutched herself, moaning and jerking her hips as she reached an intense climax. She closed her eyes and grimaced. "Ah yes," she murmured, as the spasms subsided. She leaned against the table, breathing deeply.

After a long moment she recovered her self-control. She brushed her hair back from her face, closed the waistband of her pants, and turned her attention back to him. "You're here," she told Aton, "for a simple operation." She picked up a wad of rags, mopped up some of the blood flowing from the wounds that she had inflicted, then tossed the rags aside. "Have you ever heard of the dorsal nerves?" She touched the area immediately above his penis. "Right here under the pudendal bone. They transmit sensation from your genitals to your brain."

Aton shook his head. His pulse was still hammering, and he was bathed in nervous sweat.

"If those nerves are damaged—if they are crushed, for example—you can no longer feel anything from your genitals. Understand?" She watched him, obviously enjoying the effects that her words were having.

Aton's stomach heaved, and he felt a sudden urge to vomit.

"A man can still get erect, of course, by indirect stimulation—thinking about sex, or maybe looking at a woman's body. But without that nerve, he can't feel any direct sensations from his penis. And if you don't have those sensations, you can't come. Isn't that right?" She raised an eyebrow.

Aton could remain silent no more. "You're sick," he said in a shaky voice. "If I ever get my hands on you, you'll suffer. I swear to god." He broke off, trembling with fear and rage.

"Good, Aton. Very good." She moved closer and patted his cheek. "You want revenge, don't you? You want to hurt people. You want to make them pay for all the suffering you've endured. I can see now you'll be very useful to us." She drew back from him and shook her head. "Still, the operation does need to be done."

She picked up a bottle of colorless liquid, pulled out its stopper, and moistened a wad of gauze. Aton smelled raw alcohol, then felt a cold caress as she wiped it across his lower abdomen.

"Oh god," he moaned.

"There's no god to help you here, Aton. Don't you remember what Oris told you? You belong to us now. We are your god. You must worship us, love us, and obey us, for there is none other." She picked up a scalpel. "Try not to move. This is a delicate procedure and I don't want to damage you more than necessary."

He lay rigid, knowing there was no way to prevent what she was going to do. He closed his eyes. The blade sliced cleanly into his flesh. Then he felt instruments prick and probe inside him, and there was a sudden flash of overwhelming, stabbing agony. He let out a despairing cry. Mercifully, he fainted.

29.

He regained consciousness as she was sewing the wound. "Hurts," he mumbled. Forgetting where he was, he tried to move—but the straps still held him down.

She knotted the thread and cut it, then replaced her surgical tools on the shelf beside him. Her fingers were wet with blood.

"You did it to me," he said, realizing the terrible reality of what had just happened.

"Yes." She turned away. "You can rest now." She wiped her hands and walked out of the room.

He lay on the table feeling pain throbbing from the incision that she had made. He stared at the rough-hewn wooden ceiling. Should he feel horror and anguish at what had happened? For some reason, he felt only a sense of dull despair. He was drained, weak, and thankful that for the time being, the torture was over.

"I told you," Garvin's voice came from the bed opposite. "I said you'd live."

Aton didn't bother to reply.

Later, one of the guards came in with a bowl of gruel. The straps holding Aton were becoming painful, cutting off circulation to his legs and arms, and his body chafed where it pressed against the rough table beneath him. But when he asked the woman if he could sit up to drink the soup, she said nothing. She spooned it into his mouth mechanically, then walked away.

"They ain't finished with you yet," said Garvin.

Aton turned and looked at the man. "What do you mean?"

The door of the infirmary opened and four guards marched in. They took hold of the corners of the table where Aton lay and lifted it off the frame beneath. Holding it like a stretcher, with Aton still strapped to it on his back, they carried it outside.

He winced and blinked in the bright sunlight. "What's happening?" His voice sounding weak and hoarse. "Where are you taking me?"

They carried him into a long building lined with tiers of wooden bunks. Warriors stood in two lines on either side. All of them had hideously scarred, ravaged faces. They stared down at him impassively as he was carried past them. No one spoke.

He felt a renewed sense of dread as the board tilted under him. The guards rested the bottom end of it on the floor and leaned the top end against the wall. Aton found himself held upright, facing back the way he had come. He turned his head and found Oris standing to his right, Quentain to his left. Beside her was a big ceramic bowl full of glowing coals. Metal implements, like small branding irons, were resting in it.

Aton shut his eyes. He moaned.

"Today this man becomes one of us," Oris said. Her voice was loud; it seemed to fill the long room. "His links with his past life have been cut. We will mark him now as one of our own. Baz, you first."

"No!" Aton shouted.

The warrior stepped forward. His ruined face twisted in a little rictus of contempt as he looked at Aton.

"The marking stone," said Oris. She held out a large wedge-shaped flint that had one sharp, jagged edge. Baz took it from her.

"Proceed," said Oris.

Baz grimaced with simple, vicious bloodlust. He drew back his arm, then smashed the sharpened edge of the flint into Aton's face.

Blood welled up and started flowing. Quentain grabbed Aton's hair to hold his head steady, picked up one of the irons, and pressed its red-hot tip into the wound. There was a sizzling sound followed by a stench of burning flesh. Aton writhed in his bonds. He heard himself screaming; his whole world was turning black with pain.

"Next," said Oris.

Another warrior walked in front of Aton. The marking stone was passed to him. He gouged it into Aton's chest. Again, Quentain cauterized the wound to staunch the flow of blood.

"Next."

Altogether, there were more than two hundred warriors.

Aton was unconscious long before they finished with him.

30.

For a while he was in shock. They strapped him loosely to a bed in the infirmary, and he lay there shivering, muffled in blankets. Later, he became feverish. He screamed and mumbled and cried, then pissed with fear when Quentain came to examine him.

On the second day the fever broke. He became fully conscious, and one of the guards came to feed him. He managed to swallow some soup, but felt frighteningly weak. The burns all over his face and chest were hideously painful.

Garvin was still lying in the next bed. "Like I said before, you'll live," he told Aton after the guard had left. "You been through the worst, now."

Aton stared at the man, no longer knowing who, if anyone, he should trust.

Garvin laughed. "That's right, meat, don't believe it. Don't believe nothing anyone says. 'Cause no one's got friends here. None."

"None?" Aton repeated dumbly.

"Me and Baz, we was sort of buddies. That's why they sent him out to bring me in. They turn guys against each other. That's the way they work."

Aton closed his eyes. He didn't want to hear any more.

"Just don't do what I did," said Garvin. "Don't think you can get away with something. 'Cause you can't. If the women don't get you, the dorgs will."

Aton subsided into sleep. He dreamed formlessly of torture and pain, and woke in a cold sweat to find

another of the guards bending over him. He shouted
in fear and cringed away from her—but she was
merely bringing him something more to eat. This time,
she freed one of his arms and he was able to consume
solid food.

"Garvin?" he asked, turning toward the man.

But the next bed was empty.

"He's outside," said the guard, taking the empty
bowl out of Aton's hands. "Take a look."

Aton blinked. "Outside?"

"Come on." She unstrapped his other arm. Slowly,
shakily, he swung his legs out of bed and managed to
stand. She helped him to the window, and he rested
there. It provided him with an unobstructed view of
the yard.

Everyone in the camp had gathered in a big circle.
Warriors stood shoulder to shoulder with their arms
folded. Men from the work gang sat in front of them
in the dirt. Guards and their dorgs occupied strategic
positions around the perimeter.

At the center of the circle, a massive stake had been
driven into the ground. Garvin's wrists had been tied
together and secured to a metal ring above his head.
His ankles, too, were tied. He had been stripped naked.

Quentain was standing in front of him holding a
leather sack. It seemed to writhe with a life of its own.
As Aton watched, she reached into it, pulled out a
small, wriggling object, and attached it to Garvin's
body.

Aton recognized it as one of the leechworms that
had fastened themselves to him when Malice had first
abandoned him out in the jungle clearing. He turned
away as Garvin started to scream. "That's all there is
here," he muttered, slumping back into bed. "Pain."

The woman secured his wrists to the bedframe. "You
do what you're told, you don't get hurt. You break the
rules, we break you."

She took the empty bowl and left.

31.

Over the next two days, Aton slowly regained his strength. Meanwhile, out in the yard, Garvin slowly died. For hours at a stretch he would be left unmolested. Sometimes they would even force-feed him and pick off a few of the parasites covering his body. But then Quentain would visit him with some new, deviously cruel torture, and his screams would start again.

On the third day, when Garvin finally died, Baz came to visit Aton in the infirmary. The big warrior walked in unannounced, stopped at the foot of Aton's bed, and stood there studying him.

Aton said nothing. He waited, feeling renewed fear.

"You're ugly as me, now, meat," Baz said finally. "Maybe worse."

Still Aton waited.

Baz laughed. It was a scornful, ugly sound. "All right, meat. I come to take you out of here."

Aton jerked back from the man. "Why? What for?"

"The rough stuff is all over." Baz unbuckled the straps holding Aton's wrists. "You're one of us now, meat."

Aton stood up. He still had only half his strength, and the wounds on his face and chest were a mess of pus and mucus. "There's no more torture?"

"Not unless you go looking for it, like Garvin did." Baz shook his head and spat on the floor. "Stupid bastard. Listen, Five, I'm the commander, understand? You do what I say, you keep out of trouble. But you don't call me 'sir.' None of that shit. This ain't like a normal kind of army."

"Then what is it?"

"Oris can tell it to you better than me. Come on." He grabbed Aton's arm and hustled him out of the building.

They walked across the center of the yard. Aton felt dizzy and disoriented to be out in the open. Two guards were cutting the ropes that still supported Garvin's lifeless body. Aton averted his eyes, but he heard the furious buzzing of flies covering the corpse, and there was no way he could avoid the stench of Garvin's excrement and his rotting flesh.

Baz led Aton to the barracks where the initiation ceremony had been conducted. No men were in it now; the bunks stood in empty lines. There was still a sense of violence there, though, and Aton had to fight his instinct to turn and run.

"This one's yours," said Baz, pointing to a bunk near the door. He pulled a sack out from under it, untied the neck, and emptied it onto the mattress. "Blanket. Bowl. Spoon. Rope. Gloves. Leather breeches, jacket. Sandals. Dagger, club, sword and sheath."

Aton stared at the items, then looked up at the warrior uncomprehendingly. "You're giving me weapons?"

Baz moved closer, till his face was less than a foot away. "You saw what happened to Garvin. That's nothing compared to what would happen to you, meat, if you tried to do harm to one of the women. Or me, for that matter."

Aton looked back at the weapons. He said nothing.

"You're thinking maybe you wouldn't get caught?" Baz laughed. "The dorgs is smarter than you think. Even the women is scared of 'em."

Aton absorbed the information silently.

Baz shook his head. "I don't like a man who don't say much, Five. What's on your mind? Revenge, is it?"

Aton drew a slow breath. "After what they did to me, it's only natural, isn't it?"

"All right," said Baz. He rested his knuckles on his hips. "Let's think about it. Supposing you get past the guards to Oris somehow, and kill her. Assuming you aim to stay alive, you got to get the hell out, right? So, where you gonna go? We're in the middle of a thousand miles of jungle. But even supposing you get through to some sort of civilization, who's gonna want to know you? Your face looks like shit, and when it's healed up, it won't look much better. And Quentain sliced you up so you can't fuck. You're *different* now, get it? There's no going back. You're one of us, meat, and this is your whole life, here in this camp."

"I see." Aton's face remained blank.

Baz laughed. He punched Aton's shoulder. "Five, you're a stubborn son of a bitch, and you got a lot of hate locked up in there. We can use that. We got all kinds of ways to get it out of your system. But do it my way, eh? You want to kill something, you want to hear something scream, it can be arranged. Just ask me first."

Aton shook his head, disturbed by the emotions that Baz's words evoked. He was appalled by the idea that he should inflict the kind of pain on others that had been inflicted on him. But—if Oris or Quentain were helpless in front of him right now, would he show them any mercy? Likewise, the warriors who had scarred him. They, too, should pay for what they had done. Including Baz. And as for outsiders . . . he realized he didn't care for their well-being, either. He hated them for not being mutilated as he had been.

He picked up the sword and hefted it. He imagined thrusting the blade into soft, warm flesh. The thought made him shudder—with revulsion, and with lust.

"All right, Five." Baz pointed his finger in Aton's face. "Just remember two things. Number one: watch your ass. You drop your guard, you're liable to get hurt. Some of the guys is kill-crazy, understand? Which brings me to point two: don't trust nobody. Nobody, understand? And that includes me." He gave Aton a hideous grin.

Aton was still holding the sword. For a moment, he imagined turning it on himself. After all, what Baz said was true: there was no other life now outside of this camp. And that barely seemed worth living.

Still, there was unfinished business. He had no intention of dying so long as Oris, Quentain, and his other enemies were still alive.

"Stow it," Baz said, nodding toward the sword, "and pack your stuff back under the bed."

Slowly, Aton did so.

"Right. Now, Oris wants to see you. She got some stuff to tell you. You know where her cabin is. I got to go check on a dorg that they been training for you." He nodded to Aton. "See you in a bit."

Aton stood and watched dumbly as Baz walked out and left him alone in the barracks. To be suddenly unsupervised was disorienting. He glanced around, almost expecting to find someone watching him; but the big room was completely empty.

Aton walked out into the sunlight and surveyed the yard. Garvin's body had been dragged away, and none of the guards was currently visible. He looked toward the gate. It was open—but just beyond it, he knew, were the guards with their dorgs. Beyond them, the pit of poisonous, carnivorous plants; and beyond that, the jungle. His sense of sudden freedom was an illusion. He was still a prisoner, and his only rational option was to obey his masters.

32.

One of Oris's guards escorted him up to her room. It was exactly as he remembered it, with a single exception—one of the torture devices was now occupied. A naked figure lay stretched out flat on a wooden table. The victim's head was covered with a canvas hood. On top of the body was a long, wide plank of wood studded with long spikes that pointed downward. Rocks had been piled onto the plant to increase the pressure. Blood trickled across the victim's skin from the dozens of deep puncture wounds and dripped onto the floor below.

Aton hesitated, staring at the tableau and feeling a confused mixture of emotions. The guard grabbed his arm impatiently and hustled him past. "Kneel," she reminded him as he reached the table where Oris sat.

Aton fell to his knees. The sight of Oris now triggered a reflex of unthinking fear, in the knowledge of her power to inflict torture upon him. But at the same time, following on the heels of the fear, he felt hate and a twisted, hungry lust for revenge. The emotions surged in him, making him tremble as he kneeled before her.

Oris surveryed him briefly. "Here, Five." She picked up something from the desk and held it out to him.

Clumsily, he took it from her. It was a mirror. For the first time, he saw the damage to his face.

"Hold him," Oris snapped to the guard, as Aton started to sway.

"No." He pulled back, not wanting the guard to

touch him. "I'm all right." Quickly, he placed the mirror back on the table.

Oris nodded slowly. "You've been marked, Five. You are now one of us. Soon you will break your last link with your past life. And after that, you will be a warrior."

Aton waited. He said nothing.

"You're come to see me now," she went on, "to learn about the camp here. There are no secrets; now that you've been initiated, you can know the facts."

She spoke casually, conversationally. He listened, and he understood. But this was the woman who had defiled his body. How could she talk to him so casually? How could he kneel passively and listen? He saw himself gouging her face with his bare fingernails and ripping at her breasts.

"I expect you've wondered about the underlying purpose of this camp," Oris was saying.

Dumbly, Aton nodded.

She leaned back in her chair and clasped her hands on the table in front of her. "We are creating the ultimate warrior." Her dark eyes stared broodingly at him, and her face was intensely serious. "Other armies, throughout history, have tried to pretend they could remain civilized while killing their enemies. They invented codes of military honor, rules of combat, procedures for the care of prisoners." She grimaced and gestured dismissively. "To kill is not civilized. Anyone who pretends it can be is a hypocrite, trying to save his own conscience. No, war is barbaric, and the more barbaric warriors are, the more effective they will be." She scrutinized Aton. "Does the concept bother you, Five? You may speak. There are no restrictions in this meeting."

He drew a slow, shaky breath. "Without some limits or some code to live by," he said, "a soldier ceases to be human."

"Precisely." Oris looked quietly, cruelly pleased. "Our warriors are not human. They are fanatics driven by frustration and hate. Frustration, because all their sexual energies must be sublimated into violence. Hate, because they hate themselves for being deformed, and they hate the enemy for being whole."

Aton felt himself trembling again. He closed his eyes for a moment, struggling for control. The rage and fear threatened to overwhelm him. He felt terror at what she had done. He longed to ruin this woman as she had ruined him.

Oris nodded knowingly. "Yes, Aton, you have been brutalized. I have been cruel and inhuman. I have ruined you. But that is my right. *You are my possession*, do you understand? When you walked into this camp, you surrendered to me and became my slave. I will continue to do anything I want to you. Anything. Remember that."

He nodded wordlessly. One day, one day, he would have the power over her that she now had over him. He clung to that thought, no matter how impossible it seemed.

"Do you want to know what happens next?" she asked.

He nodded again, not trusting himself to speak.

"You will be trained. And then you will fight. No, not here on Chthon; when the time comes, you'll be transported offworld. Don't be deceived by the primitive conditions here; we have access to interstellar transport. This camp is for training; it serves no other purpose." She paused, allowing Aton time to assimilate everything she had said. "All right, Five. If you have any questions, you may ask them."

He was silent for a long moment, trying to organize his thoughts. "This really is Chthon?" he asked.

"Yes. We are in the undeveloped hemisphere. Originally, as I told you, we were imprisoned underground. We emerged into Idyllia, on the other side of the planet. Some of us then chose to retreat here. Others were . . . persuaded to join us."

"I see." It sounded as if it was true. He decided he

might as well be truthful with her, in turn. "There are some things you may not know about me," he said. "I was part of the Federation force that liberated your people."

"Yes. I discovered that recently. We do have communications equipment here. I checked on you, Five, after you were first brought in. Your name is listed in Federation records. I know your role." She shrugged. "If you think you deserve special treatment because you gave us our freedom, you're wrong. I owe you nothing. You were stupid to release us. Now you are paying for your stupidity. You are a slave here, like any other. You will serve me, or you will suffer."

He stared at her. Her cruel face seemed to resonate in his memories. He recalled his nightmare, which in retrospect seemed so horribly predictive. "I have a sense," he said, "that we met once before."

She shook her head. "No. Is that all, Five?"

He sighed. "There is one other thing. Last time I was here, you said you'd look after the emp. The creature that I had with me. I suppose there's no chance—"

"I told you that I always speak the truth." She stood up. "I said you would see that animal again, alive, and you will. We can take care of that right now. Come with me."

33.

They took him to the guardhouse. It was just as he remembered it, except that the prisoner who had been moaning the last time he had been here was now silent. There was a rancid, acrid smell. Aton wondered if the man had died in his cell and been left to rot.

Oris waited while one of her guards went to the first of the cells and unlocked its massive wooden door. The woman disappeared inside, then emerged carrying a small bundle of fur.

"Give that to him." Oris pointed to Aton.

At the sight of the animal, Aton felt a surge of sweet emotion. Concern, affection, and simple pleasure—it was a sudden, unexpected antidote to all the fear and hate. He reached out. "Here, emp!"

The ball of fur stirred sluggishly. A small black face blinked up at him. It looked feeble and listless. "Aton," it said in a small voice.

"Here. Come on." He lifted it onto his chest.

Contact with him seemed to revive it. "Aton," it said again. It clung to him and nuzzled him.

He stroked it. Its body felt thin, and its fur was dry and dull. "It's okay now," he said. "You'll be okay."

"You will agree that I kept my word," Oris said.

He turned toward her. "Yes. You did."

"All right, we have one more thing to take care of. Come with me."

He hesitated. "I can bring the emp?"

She shrugged. "It seems marginally intelligent; it

might actually be useful." She turned and walked out of the guardhouse.

Aton followed her across the central yard, with her guards walking either side of him. "Feel better now?" Aton asked the emp.

"Happy." It climbed higher and moved around to his shoulders. Its little face turned one way, then the other, blinking in the sunlight.

Oris led the way to the far corner of the camp. There was an area here enclosed by a high wall of logs stacked one upon another. Narrow gaps had been cut halfway up the wall, forming crude windows into the enclosure.

Baz was standing there. He beckoned to Aton. "Hey, been waiting for you." He gestured to the nearest of the windows. "Got something to show you."

Cautiously, Aton peered in. He saw a wide, deep pit containing a half-dozen dorgs that were not yet fully grown. They were growling and pouncing, lashing one another with their spiked tails, seizing each other's heads in their fearsome jaws. At first it looked as if they were trying to rip each other to pieces. Then Aton realized that this was their idea of play.

The emp moved nervously on Aton's shoulders. "Bad," it said.

"See the big one there?" Baz said. "That one's gonna be yours. I been checking on it. It comes out the day after tomorrow. It's a mean son of a bitch."

"I see." Aton stepped back. He stroked the emp, trying to calm it.

Baz put his fingers in his mouth and whistled. The biggest dorg turned and stared in his direction, then came bounding across. It got up on its hind legs and pressed its nose against the gap in the wall where Baz was standing. It made snuffling noises and growled softly, staring out with slitted yellow eyes.

"A warrior's dorg is his only true friend," said Oris. "It's highly intelligent, and it will die to defend him.

At the same time, if it sees its master behaving in a way that is inappropriate, it will turn on him instantly."

Aton looked at Oris. "What do you mean by 'inappropriate'?"

"If you show weakness. If you desert your comrades. If you disobey my orders. If you attempt to escape. The dorg will not kill you; more usually, it will seize you by your legs and drag you to me for proper discipline."

"The only way Garvin got out was on account of his dorg got hurt," Baz explained. "Dorg broke its leg, so Garvin was on his own a couple days." He squinted at the emp, which was hiding behind Aton's shoulder from the dorg and making little whimpering noises. "That's the critter you had when I found you, right?"

"Right," said Aton.

"Give him to me a minute, so's you can get closer to the dorg there. He needs to sniff you, see? Get familiar with you."

Aton hesitated.

"Do as Baz says," said Oris. She spoke flatly and firmly, leaving no doubt that this was a command.

Aton disengaged the emp from his back and handed it to Baz. The emp chittered uncertainly, looking from one man to the other.

Baz bundled its thin body so he could hold it in one hand. Quickly, before Aton could intervene, he drew back his arm and threw the emp up and over the wooden rail, into the dorgs' compound.

Aton stared transfixed. The emp screeched in fear. It flattened itself and tried to glide beyond the fence at the opposite side of the compound. But the fence was too high. The emp hit it and fell, scrabbling with its little claws. Halfway down, it got a grip and hung there. But the dorgs had seen it. One of them leaped up and grabbed it in its front paws. Savage, serrated claws skewered the emp's small body. It wailed in pain and terror as the dorg dragged it down. There was a chorus of growls and the dorgs scuffled in the dirt,

ripping the emp apart and devouring it with awful
ripping, crunching sounds. Within moments, nothing
was left but a few tufts of fur and spatters of blood.

"Hold him!" Oris shouted to her guards as Aton
threw himself at Baz. They seized him by the arms,
but he was hardly aware of them. He flung one off,
kicked the other in the groin, and grabbed Baz by the
throat.

"I said hold him!"

This time four of her guards caught Aton and dragged
him back. He kicked and writhed, possessed by a fit of
rage so intense he could hardly see.

Oris stepped in front of him. "Stop struggling."
Quickly, she slapped his face. "I said *stop!*"

The order cut through his anger. Slowly, as he realized there was no way to free himself, his tantrum
subsided. He gasped for breath, his heart pounding.
Once more he saw the little emp being shredded by
the black beasts in their pen. "You bastard." He looked
at Baz with a terrible mixture of rage and grief. "Why?
Why did you do that?"

Baz shrugged. "I got my orders, is why. I told you,
meat, don't trust nobody. Not even me."

"Every man cares about something or someone,"
Oris explained quietly. "Maybe he's devoted to a friend
or a person in his family. Maybe he loves a special
place where he likes to go, or he has something he
likes to do that gives him special pleasure. Unfortunately, we cannot permit love, devotion, or pleasure
here. Those emotions give too much comfort, and
they link a man to his civilized past. They inhibit his
need to kill. So we make it our business to find that
one most special thing which a man cares about, and
when we find it, we destroy it, so that he can never
have it again."

"I hate you," Aton sobbed. "God, I hate you."

"Good, Aton. Very good. You have lost everything
now, and hate is all you have left." She smiled cruelly.
"You have become a warrior."

34.

During the next month, they trained him.

He was already strong from growing up on the high-gravity world of Hvee. He already possessed martial-arts skills that he had learned in his youth. He already had a natural tendency toward aggression, thanks to his Minion blood.

They subjected him to tests of strength and stamina, and punished him when he failed. They sharpened his reflexes by making him fight to survive, and they showed him all the ways to kill with a blade, a club, or even a fist. Most of all, they taught him the pure pleasure that could come not merely from causing pain, but from causing death.

The training period was a mosaic of challenges and confrontations, bruises and blood. Each day began with aching muscles and a dull loathing for himself and his new life. Each day ended with weary satisfaction at his growing ability to conquer his environment and his adversaries.

Some men in the barracks tried to befriend him. He was not deceived; they all had ulterior motives, for they were all as grim and mean as he was.

Others tried to intimidate him. These he would fight without hesitation, regardless of his own safety. If he was able to inflict even a small wound, he was quite willing to sustain almost any degree of physical damage himself. Nothing could be worse than the pain he had already experienced. By comparison, the satisfaction of revenge was infinite.

At the end of the first month, he was left with a jumble of memories. . . .

His dorg was securely muzzled, and they blunted its claws and the spines on its tail. Aton was fitted with leather body armor and thrown into a pit with the animal, which now weighed more than he did and was twice as strong. The pit was only ten feet across and contained no tools or weapons. Aton was told that he would not be allowed out until either he was unconscious or the dorg was beaten into submission.

The beast hit him savagely with its forearms, lashed him with its tail, and ripped pieces off his armor with its blunted claws. He head-butted it, to no avail. He tried to seize its genitals, but found they were protected in a pouch that retracted into its body. Finally, dazed and desperate, he rammed a piece of his broken armor through the mesh of its muzzle and wedged its jaws open. He then thrust his arm into the creature's mouth and mauled its throat with his fingernails. It writhed in pain, retched, and almost choked to death on its vomit.

After that, the dorg treated him with guarded respect. He, meanwhile, dreamed of finding a way to immobilize it somehow, so that he could torture it slowly to death. He would never forget what it and its kin had done to the emp.

A warrior named Knize was the undisputed expert with a broadsword. He and Aton sparred with swords wrapped in cloth, their points enclosed in protective wooden tips to prevent serious injuries. Aton soon realized that he would never equal Knize's technique; the man had spent a lifetime perfecting his skills and had a unique talent, which Aton respected.

His bragging, however, and the way he openly despised his opponents were intolerable. Before one of their matches, Aton secretly removed most of the nails securing the heel of Knize's boot to its sole. He suggested then that they fight in a stony area of the compound, where the footing was uneven. Always willing to accept a challenge, Knize agreed.

When the heel twisted off his boot and he fell, Aton was ready. He slashed his blunted sword across the front of Knize's throat.

His larynx was permanently damaged. He never bragged again.

Aton later explained to Baz that the whole thing had been a regrettable accident.

The warriors ate together in the barracks. During his first week with the group, Aton found himself sitting between Tyson and Ormar, two of the largest, meanest men. Tyson, on the left, elbowed him sharply in the ribs. Aton turned; Tyson grinned and apologized. Aton looked back at his plate and found one chunk of meat missing.

He turned to Ormar, on his right. The man's mouth was full, although his own plate hadn't been touched.

Aton spat into the remaining food on his plate and pushed it across in front of Ormar. "Here," he said. "Have some more."

Ormar scowled at him. He knocked Aton's plate aside and made a gruff warning sound.

"Maybe you'd prefer something to drink," said Aton. A mug of hot tea was in front of him. He picked it up and threw it in the big man's face, scalding him.

A few minutes later, when Baz broke up the brawl, Ormar was methodically punching Aton in the ribs while Tyson held his arms behind him. Aton refused to explain how the fight had started.

Any gratuitous violence between warriors was discouraged. For his attack on Ormar, Aton was sentenced to a day with the work gang.

The labor was intolerably hard. Worse, he was tormented by knowing that it was almost certainly unnecessary. If the warriors were going to fight their

battles offworld, there was no need to fortify the camp.
The job, he suspected, existed purely as a punishment
and as a test of endurance.

He hated the rocks that he was forced to haul, hated
the guards who supervised him and whipped his
naked back, and hated the men he worked with. Some
of them were warriors like himself, being punished for
petty crimes. Most, however, were too weak or timid
to be admitted to the warrior class. They were in the
gang as a final test of survival. If the work didn't break
them, they might yet earn warrior status. Otherwise,
they would be discarded.

Aton felt degraded to be surrounded by these men.
They disgusted him.

He found a pebble that was almost perfectly round
and hid it in the waistband of his breeches till none of
the guards was looking his way. Surreptitiously, he
rolled it under the foot of a man climbing to the top of
the wall, carrying a massive rock on his shoulders.

The man's foot slipped from under him. He fell
twenty feet to the ground, and the rock that he had
been carrying landed on top of him, breaking his back.
He lay there screaming in agony.

Aton volunteered to deal with the problem, and the
guard agreed. Aton threw the man into the trench of
carnivorous plants. It took two hours for their acids to
kill him, and he continued to scream for most of that
time. Occasionally Aton would glance down and see
him trapped in the plant's mouth, struggling feebly.

Aton was sent outside the camp to hunt game under
the supervision of Baz and their two dorgs. Baz reluctantly told Aton all he knew about the wildlife of
Chthon—reluctantly, because he would have probably
derived some quiet satisfaction from seeing Aton in-
jured or killed by the plants and predators of the
jungle.

Hunting was easy with the dorgs to help. The massive black creatures—part cat, part wolf, part lizard—

were indefatigable killing machines. Sometimes, though, they seemed to hold back deliberately so that the men would have to use their fighting skills.

Baz cornered a creature the size and shape of a small alligator with four short, stumpy legs and a long, thin body. The body was pink, and the head was round with large, pale eyes.

The creature seemed timid. It tried to run for cover in a nearby swamp. Baz used his rope as a lasso and dragged it out by the neck. Rather than kill it straight-away, however, he tied it to a nearby tree. "Listen to this," he said, drawing his dagger.

For the next half hour he made small cuts in the creature's plump, pink body, torturing it to death. Its screams were eerily human. When Aton closed his eyes, he could almost imagine that it was a woman crying out in pain—or ecstasy.

As the animal cried and writhed and bled, Baz's breathing became labored. His face turned red and his hands started to shake. Finally he fell upon the animal in incoherent fury, rubbing his body against it while he stabbed it repeatedly in the belly.

He groaned, stiffened, then slumped against the creature, gasping for breath. When he pulled back, there was a wet stain in the front of his breeches. "It ain't much," he said to Aton, shaking his head and grimacing. "But it's better than nothing."

On Aton's next trip into the jungle it was his turn to hunt and kill one of the screaming creatures. Like Baz, he found it gave him satisfaction which he could no longer achieve any other way. Unfortunately, however, it also left him craving more.

All of the warriors had suffered Quentain's opera-tion on their dorsal nerves. They could become aroused by sexual fantasies, and their organs could become erect, but when they touched themselves they felt nothing.

Sex was a constant obsession, all the more because

it was unavailable. Barracks-room gossip often centered on the female guards and what the warriors would do to them if, somehow, they ever had the chance. It was pure fantasy, of course; during the day, the women had their dorgs to protect them, and each night one of the huge black animals was stationed inside the barracks building, lying just inside the door to keep watch on the warriors while they slept.

Baz said it was pointless even to think about having sex with the women at the camp. He claimed that with the exception of Oris and Quentain, they weren't capable of it. He said he had once seen one of the female guards naked, and her chest had been flat, she'd had no pubic hair, nor any genitals, so far as he could tell.

Aton was interested in Baz's story—not because he thought it was true, but because the inhumanity of the guards puzzled him. Their only emotions seemed to be anger and hate, and unlike Oris and Quentain, they never showed any kind of physicality toward their prisoners or each other. He decided to find out for himself what they looked like under their clothes, and started to evolve a plan. The more he thought about it, the more ambitious it became.

It was impossible, though, unless he could evade the dorg that stood guard each night. Aton imagined various ways of killing it—then remembered the soup that had made him drowsy on the night when Oris and Quentain had used him sexually. Everything that the warriors ate was harvested from the jungle of Chthon, so the herb that had sedated him was probably no exception. On his next hunting trip he quietly gathered a variety of plants. Over the next few days he sampled them till he found one that had soporific effects.

He waited till there was a moonless night, then mixed the herb into food that was fed to the barracks dorg. After an hour, the animal seemed to fall asleep. Aton allowed another hour to be sure, then crept past it and waited outside the barracks in the darkness.

There were regular guard patrols. He seized the first
woman who came by, wrapped a length of rope around
her neck, and throttled her till she was unconscious.
Quickly, then, he used his dagger to cut her clothes
off.

Aton stopped and stared in wonder at the woman's
body. Baz had been right: her chest was as flat as a
man's, with nipples that were little more than pimples.
The skin between her legs was completely smooth,
with no sign of a vaginal opening. Either she had
undergone some operation, or she was the product of
some perverse gene splice. Either way, she was the
female equivalent of a eunuch.

Aton felt a sudden spasm of anger. Touching and
stripping her had aroused him to an almost unbearable degree—and now he had no outlet for his lust.
Crazed with frustration, he raped her anally, even
though his own genitals were dead to all sensation.
She regained consciousness during the act and started
to struggle. When he looked down at her, he imagined
he saw Oris's face. He lost his sanity and stabbed her
in the stomach with his dagger. Her death throes were
erotic to him. He came as she died.

Slowly, he regained his senses. He realized that the
next guard patrol would soon be due, and would discover what had happened. His clothes were stained
with the woman's blood.

He crept back into the barracks past the drugged
dorg, and quietly roused Baz while the warriors nearby
slept undisturbed. The commander was suspicious, but
when Aton told him that the dorg seemed sickly and a
woman guard was dead outside, he had to investigate.

Aton waited till Baz was bending over the guard,
then slew him with his sword. He crept back into the
barracks, transferred his incriminating collection of
herbs to Baz's kit bag, then hurried back outside and
shouted for help.

Oris commended him, and he was promoted: he
took the place of the dead commander.

*   *   *

One morning Aton found a dozen strangers lying unconscious in the yard outside. They were bound hand and foot and seemed to have been drugged. Guards were carrying them away on stretchers.

Rumor had it that all of the newcomers had been abducted from Idyllia. Aton realized there was only one way they could have been brought from there to the camp unobtrusively during the night: by a transit vehicle with a grav-drive.

The first of the men died from shock on Quentain's operating table. The second was considered too physically weak to be a warrior and was thrown into the work gang.

The third was a man named Peck. He had a body like a weightlifter, broad-shouldered, heavily muscled, and deeply tanned. His face was handsome and boyish, with clear blue eyes and curly blond hair.

After Quentain had operated on him he was brought into the barracks for the initiation ceremony. Aton, as the new commander, stood first in line. He stepped forward, took the marking stone from Oris, and weighed it in his hand for a moment, studying the handsome golden-haired man in front of him. Meditatively, he pinched the man's cheek and pulled, stretching it outward from his face. The handsome one whimpered and tried to pull free, but Aton tightened his grip, digging in his nails. With cold satisfaction, he raised the marking stone and used its sharp edge to saw all the way through the extended web of skin. The man screamed, blood started flowing freely, and Quentain raised her iron to cauterize the wound. Aton turned calmly and passed the stone to the next man in line. He examined the fragment of skin he still held between finger and thumb, and then tossed it idly aside.

Near the end of his first month as a warrior, Aton woke suddenly in the middle of the night. He was unsure what had roused him. The only sound in the barracks was the snoring of the men in their bunks.

Then he felt something touch his mind: the same wise, gentle intelligence that he had sensed twice before. "We are concerned," the voice seemed to say. "You have suffered. You are sick. You need help."

Something about the invasion of his sleep by this patronizing intelligence angered him. *Who are you and where are you?* he thought.

There was a pause, as if the entity was disconcerted by the hostility it sensed in him. "We are mineral entities beyond your galaxy. Once we collaborated with the plasma intelligence of Chthon. That was in another timeline, another universe.* Later, we realized our error, and worked to undo what had been done.** We saved you, then, from death in that timeline, brought you to this one, and helped you to destroy Chthon's evil core. But now we see our debt still remains unpaid. Chthon's mind still lives. Again we must try to help."

If you have the power to help me, why didn't you do anything before? Why did you let them capture me here?

Another pause, as they assimilated his response. "We tried to warn you, in your dreams, when you were on Hvee. We showed you the death of Malice. We showed you your future with Oris."

You put those dreams in my head?

"As a warning—"

Get out of my mind and leave me alone, Aton thought savagely. *Stay the fuck away from me, do you understand?*

The entity seemed to recoil in distress. He felt its presence diminish. Then it was gone, as silently as it had come, and he was alone again with his own thoughts of anger and revenge.

---

*Author's note: As described in *Phthor*.
**Author's note: As described in *Plasm*.

35.

Aton was sweating under the patchwork of his leather armor, and his dorg was panting in the heat. As he passed beneath some overhanging branches a tomato-pod dropped its feeding tentacle toward him. He sensed it before he saw it, and slashed it with his sword. Killing the local wildlife had long since become a reflex.

The severed tentacle fell to the ground and writhed like a snake with its head cut off. He picked it up and stowed it in one of the heavy sacks draped across the dorg's back. As a test of his skills, he had been sent out hunting alone today, to kill as many different life forms as he could and bring back a small piece of each one. Already his dorg was moving sluggishly under the cumulative load of amputated body parts.

Aton paused, listening. There was the usual endless cacophony of jungle sounds. Hadn't he heard something else, almost lost in the din?

He turned his head slowly, trying to focus his hearing. Everything seemed normal now. He tried to recall the faint noise that had alerted him. It had been a clicking sound, like a tongue against the roof of a mouth. He couldn't think of a Chthonic creature that would make that sound. Then he realized what should have been obvious all along: the noise had not come from an animal. It had been mechanical. It was the sort of click that might come from the latch of the hatch on a small transit vehicle.

He scanned the jungle, all his senses alert now. He

studied the birds in the treetops. Several were moving his way, screeching and hopping from branch to branch. What had disturbed them?

Aton slashed his sword into the undergrowth and forced his way through a thorn thicket. His dorg made a grumbling noise as it followed him, obviously not understanding the need for this excursion.

A little farther on, he found what he was looking for. He saw a gleam of silver through the foliage ahead: sunlight reflecting from curved metal.

He pushed through the undergrowth more cautiously, bending it aside instead of hacking a path. Insects buzzed around him; he ignored them. The ship was a survey vehicle, standing in a clearing just ahead.

He dropped down behind some bushes. Someone was standing outside the vehicle's exit hatch, encased in a filmy biohazard suit. The person was holding a small black ovoid, turning it to and fro. "Can't get a clean reading." It was a woman's voice. The words were muffled by the suit and diminished by distance, but Aton heard them clearly. "So much wildlife . . . thought I picked him up a moment ago, but now I'm not so sure."

Aton's skin prickled. The voice sounded eerily familiar. It stirred echoes from a past that he seldom allowed himself to think about anymore. For a moment he hesitated, unsure of what he should do.

She turned the gadget in her hands again. "Wait a minute. Now there's a reading." It was pointing directly toward him.

Aton reached a decision and stood up. Boldly, he walked toward her. He snapped his fingers, and the dorg followed.

The woman saw him emerging from the jungle and gave a little cry of surprise. She dropped the gadget she had been holding. "Aton!"

He paused, feeling disconcerted by the way that she spoke his name. "Who are you?" he demanded. Reflections in the vizor of her suit made it hard for him to see her face. "Take your helmet off."

"No. No, I'd rather not." She sounded diffident, and yet he sensed a steadfast strength as well. The combination was eerily familiar.

"Take it off!" He gestured, and the dorg padded forward, growling softly.

She flinched back from the beast, and quickly raised her hands to the helmet. "It's me. It's Alix." She fumbled with a latch and pulled the helmet over her head. "See?"

"Stay," Aton shouted to the dorg. Obediently, it slumped down onto its haunches. Aton walked past it till he was just a few feet from the woman. "Alix," he said, as if testing the word and remembering how it sounded.

Her eyes moved quickly, taking in the details of his mutilated face. "Are you all right?"

She was looking at him as if he was some sort of cripple. His grip tightened angrily on his sword. "Of course."

She glanced away, as if his defiance embarrassed her. "We were—I was concerned about you. We knew you were here, and—"

"How did you know?" he interrupted sharply.

She shook her head. "That's not important. Look, we can get you out of here right now." She gestured at the vehicle behind her, and forced herself to look back at his face. "I came here to rescue you, Aton. Do you understand?"

He eyed the ship, then turned his attention back to her. "Take me where?"

She forced an uneasy smile. "Just about anywhere you want. You see, I—I work for the Federation. In fact, I always did." The words spilled out quickly, now, as if she hoped somehow that by confessing, she might win his trust. "They posted me to Hvee, shortly after you moved there with Malice. I was told to watch over you, just in case. Even though you seemed to have killed the plasma intelligence in Chthon, there was still a possibility—"

"You mean you weren't who you said you were," Aton interjected. "You were spying on me."

She took a cautious step backward toward the ship's open hatch. One hand crept down to the leg of her suit and fumbled with a pocket flap. "I was trying to protect you," she said. "I cared about you, didn't I make that obvious? Look, I realize terrible things have happened to you, here, and—and maybe we should have come for you earlier. But whatever you've been through, Aton, it's over now. Just get in the ship, and we'll take you out of here."

He hardly heard her. He was remembering his past life on Hvee. "You gave me the emp," he said, half to himself. The memories were strange and painful, and somehow seemed alien, as if the events hadn't really happened to him at all. He had been different, then; another person entirely.

"Yes, I gave you the emp. That's how we knew where to find you. We fitted it with bioelectronic surveillance equipment. It transmitted everything back to us, including its location. But when they locked it up, and then killed it, we no longer knew what was happening. We don't know who Oris is, or exactly what she did to you, or whether the plasma intelligence is really involved. Some of my people didn't want to interfere. They didn't want to tip off anyone that we were monitoring the situation. But I finally convinced them to let me come and take you out of here." Her voice sounded plaintive and sincere. "For god's sake, Aton, don't you believe me? Don't you want to get out of this place?"

Slowly, he shook his head. "This is where I belong, now."

"No, that's just the way they want you to think, don't you see? We can repair the physical damage they did to you, we have biolabs—"

"You deceived me before. There's no reason I should trust you now."

She blinked, obviously having trouble understanding him. "Aton, I risked my life coming here to rescue you!"

He moved toward her. "Lying bitch."

She tugged something out of the pocket of her suit. A stunner. She was nervous and confused, fumbling with the safety. He kicked the weapon out of her hand. She gave a little scream and backed away from him.

He pulled out his dagger, seized the neck of her suit, and slit it open. He ripped it off her and threw her onto the ground. He searched through her suit for the transceiver she'd been speaking into earlier, and smashed it. Then he tossed the garment aside.

"Stop, Aton! Why don't you believe me?"

"Because you lied to me and used me like everyone else." He kicked her onto her back, then sat on her and started methodically shredding the rest of her clothes.

She writhed under him, seized his wrists, and tried to throw him off. She struck out at his face, and one of her fingernails drew blood. Aton swore. He slapped her head from side to side, then punched her hard in the stomach. "Lie still!" he snapped.

She coughed and gasped, staring at him with a mixture of fear and disbelief. He tore her undergarments off, tossed them aside, then stared at her body. The sight of her naked and at his mercy made Aton intensely aroused. Breathing heavily, he seized her neck between his hands and started to strangle her. Now she struggled harder. He enjoyed the way her muscles rippled as she thrashed under him, and he liked the desperate gargling noises she made at the back of her throat.

He played with her for a while. Each time she lost consciousness he relaxed his grip and allowed her to

SOMA   159

take a few frantic gulps of air. Then he put the pressure on again.

Finally, when he was on the verge of reaching his climax, he picked up his dagger. He stabbed her body repeatedly, plunging the blade savagely into her chest and abdomen. Blood pulsed out, and as she went into death spasms, he came.

He stood up, breathing heavily. He eyed her white flesh spattered with blood, then gave her lifeless body a savage kick and turned away. He wished, now, he had taken longer and inflicted more pain. But this would not be his last kill. There would be many other opportunities.

He walked into the ship. It was tiny, just built for two. He methodically smashed the communications equipment, then walked back outside.

His dorg was still there, watching and waiting. Aton drew his sword, raised it high, and brought it down with all his strength across Alix's neck. The blade cut cleanly in a single stroke. He picked up her severed head, walked to the dorg, opened the sack, and threw the head inside with the other wildlife trophies he had gathered that day. Then he turned and started back toward the camp.

36.

At first, Oris received his report impassively. As he described the details of his encounter with Alix, however, her posture changed. She sat forward in her chair and her eyes became more alert. She watched him carefully as he described murdering the woman, and she glanced at the sack lying on the floor beside him. "Show me," she said.

He rummaged among the tails, ears, limbs, and tentacles oozing blood and slime. He dragged her head out and held it up by the hair. The eyes were still staring wide, and the tongue was swollen and protruding.

"All right." Oris gestured dismissively. Evidently she had no interest in the dead woman's identity; she merely wanted to be sure that Aton had been telling the truth.

He dumped the head back in the sack.

"I'm not sure I understand why you didn't go with her," Oris said. "Even if you still wanted to avenge yourself, you could have escaped with her and killed her later."

Aton slowly shook his head. "No."

"Why not?"

He was silent for a long moment. "You told me yourself, I am part of the camp now. I am a warrior. This is where I belong. And—I still have some things that I must do." He stared at her levelly. He imagined her tied to the stake in the yard, screaming and begging while he peeled her skin off with his hunting knife. He imagined her locked in one of the torture

devices in her own room, pierced by rusty spikes and
bleeding slowly to death. He imagined immersing her
slowly, inch by inch, in a caldron of boiling water,
while he listened to her cries.

His steady stare seemed to bother her. For a fleeting moment she actually seemed unsure of herself, like
a scientist whose experiment has been so successful
that it threatens to break out of the controlled conditions of the laboratory.

Then the moment of uncertainty was gone. She
stood up. "You did the right thing, Five. I may as well
tell you, now: we were planning to pull out of the
camp in just a few more days. I can see that that
schedule will have to be accelerated. The training
period is over; it's time to apply those fighting skills.
Order your men to clean and sharpen their weapons
tonight, and have their armor in good repair."

He nodded. "Yes, Oris."

She waited, obviously expecting him to leave.

He remained kneeling before her, saying nothing.

"What is it?" she asked finally. Her face twitched in
a little tic of impatience.

"I need permission to ask a question."

"Yes?"

"Is the plasma intelligence of Chthon still alive?"

She blinked. "How should I know?" She paused.
"And why should it matter to you?"

"I just want to know," he said carefully, "who or
what is ultimately in control."

She scowled at him. "So far as you're concerned,
Five, it makes no difference." She slapped her hand
on the table. "*I'm* your master; remember that. You
live or die as I see fit. I can have you killed, maimed,
disemboweled, or whatever else I choose, if I ever
suspect you of disobeying me." She walked around
her desk and stopped close in front of him. She grabbed
his hair and jerked his head back so that he stared up
at her. "Understand?"

This was the closest he had been to her since his

initiation ceremony, when she had passed the marking stone to the men who had disfigured his face and body. He still felt a fear reflex when he remembered that scene. At the same time, kneeling in front of her, he imagined reaching quickly for the knife at his hip and thrusting it deep into her belly. The impulse was so strong he had to fight it back. Inevitably, her guard would retaliate against him. This was still not the time.

"I am your slave, Oris," he said dutifully.

"Good. Take your trophies"—she nodded toward the sack—"put your dorg in the stables, and go back to your men."

"Yes, Oris." He backed away obediently, and her guard escorted him out of the building.

His dorg was waiting in the yard. He walked with the animal to the stables and led it to its stall. "Special treat for you today," he told it.

It eyed him enigmatically. He could never tell how much human speech it understood.

Aton opened his sack and emptied it into the dorg's food bowl. The huge black animal eagerly snuffed the miscellaneous animal parts. Its tongue lapped the curdled juices. Then it seized hold of Alix's head and crunched it in its massive jaws, like a squirrel cracking a nut.

As Aton watched, he imagined how it would feel if he were four or five times his normal size, so that he would dwarf the dorg. Then, maybe, he could crush the dorg's head in *his* jaws, and smile as its blood trickled down his throat.

37.

He woke in the night to find the barracks lit with dazzling white light. It was coming from outside, high in the sky, and there was a fizzing, crackling sound like radio static. Aton ran to the window and looked out. A large interstellar passenger transport was descending, bathed in electrostatic discharge that flicked across its smooth hull like summer lightning. The glare of its landing lights illuminated the yard below and the whole compound around it, bleaching the colors and throwing stark shadows.

The ship descended slowly, its grav-drive emitting a deep, bone-rattling droning sound. The ground shook as it touched down, its bulk filling the yard.

The door of the barracks opened with a crash. "Everybody out!" shouted one of the guards. "Ten minutes, you men. Bring your kit bags. Do it!"

Already, hatches were opening and entry ramps were being lowered. Dorgs were being brought from the stables and led toward the ship. Figures hurried to and fro against the fierce glare of the floodlights.

Aton supervised the warriors as they struggled into their clothes and shouldered their bags. The men were herded across the compound by guards and their dorgs. "Up the ramp, you men. Quickly, now. Grab a bunk and strap down. Lift-off in fifteen minutes."

Food supplies were being brought from the kitchens. Extra weapons were winched in through an upper hatch. Aton glimpsed Oris directing operations, with Quentain beside her, and another figure whose features were invisible against the glaring light. The captain of the ship? There was no time for speculation.

The ship had been a pleasure cruiser. Aton and his men found themselves in pastel-colored metal corridors with concealed lighting and animated holo-murals depicting landscapes of worlds scattered across the galaxy. Aton had worked in ships like this when he had been younger, searching for Malice, but to many of the men it was a new experience. Their mutilated faces showed amazement and confusion as they inspected the luxury cabins.

"Where we headed, Five?" one of the men asked him. "What is this?"

"Just find yourself a cabin and strap down like they told you," Aton said.

"Where are we going?"

"Some other planet. I don't know where."

"What the hell for?"

He laughed. "Did you think they were teaching us to fight just for fun?"

He went back down to the main hatch and looked out. Guards were checking every building in the compound. The men in the work gang had been herded into one corner, guarded by a dozen dorgs.

"What are you doing down here, Five?" said a voice. "You should be up with your men."

Aton turned and found Oris standing beside him with one of her guards. "Just looking," he said defensively.

"Fine. You look. You're going to see something instructive." Oris turned and shouted an order to one of the guards still in the yard.

The woman went to the dorgs guarding the work gang. She slapped their flanks and gave them a command. They sprang forward at once and started savaging the crowd of fifty ragged figures.

Some of the men tried to climb the twenty-foot stockade behind them. They were dragged down. Others tried to run past the dorgs. They were tripped and mauled. The creatures seemed everywhere at once: their jaws ripped out men's throats and bit their heads off, their barbed tails lacerated men's legs, and their claws ripped and disemboweled at will.

The massacre lasted only a matter of seconds. The bloodsoaked dorgs were left wandering among the bodies, sniffing and nudging them in case any were left alive.

"That's what I do with possessions that are no longer of any use to me," Oris said calmly. "Understand?"

"Yes, Oris."

"Then go to your quarters."

He did as she said. Images of the massacre, lit by the ship's glaring lights, still swam in his eyes. He felt no pity for the men who had died. His only regret was that his enemies could not have been among them, and that he had not been the one to order the dorgs to attack.

From the viewpoint of his cabin a few minutes later, he watched as the last guards and dorgs came aboard. Almost at once, the ship's drive started and it lifted off, edging cautiously upward. There was a brief flicker of a blue particle beam, and one of the wooden buildings below burst into flame. As the ship ascended into the sky, the whole camp caught fire. The last Aton saw of it, it was burning like a beacon on its hilltop, illuminating the surrounding jungle with a flickering yellow glare.

38.

"We are heading for Xerva, a planet recently discovered near the end of one of the spiral arms." Oris was addressing the warriors in what had once been the ship's ballroom. The mean, ugly men slouched on chairs upholstered in gold and crimson beneath a dozen glittering plastic chandeliers. The ceiling showed a perpetually shifting replica of the Milky Way seen from a point above the ecliptic. The walls were ornamented with pseudo-antique heraldic crests and decorative scrollwork.

"Xerva is rich in metal deposits," she went on. "So rich, according to our data, the ores are lying on the surface for the taking. We need those metals in order to become a modern fighting force. We'll use them to build weapons."

Aton glanced at the faces of the warriors listening to her speech. He guessed that most of the men were uninterested in the details. What mattered to them was where their next meal would come from, and who they would get a chance to slaughter.

"On Chthon," Oris went on, "we had very few resources. This ship was stolen from Idyllia. The rest of our equipment we made ourselves. Fortunately, Xerva is a new colony, ill prepared to defend itself. There are only a few hundred men there, with few weapons. We will attack them with the two energy-beam emplacements on this ship. Then we will send you and the dorgs down to kill anyone who is still left alive. If we get them before they have a chance to send an SOS to the Federation, we should be able to take over and stay there without any interference for several months. By then we'll be ready to move on."

She paused, surveying the warriors. "We had to leave Chthon before we were completely ready. As a result, we have less food than we planned. We've got enough for three days of normal rations. We'll reach Xerva on the third day. If you men don't win this battle and seize the enemy's supplies, we'll all starve. You will kill, or you will die."

She turned to Aton. "If any of your warriors aren't clear about what I've said, you'll explain it to them." She turned and headed for the exit.

As soon as the men realized that the meeting was over, most of them went back to the cabins that they had commandeered. There was no group spirit in this army, no esprit de corps. They were more interested in sampling the ship's entertainments—the sense tapes and adventure videos available in the personalized units in each room. When those became boring, the men would roam the corridors, exploring the confines of the ship, defacing the luxury decor and smashing anything they felt like smashing.

The time passed slowly. The ship's lights were on constantly, as a security measure, and guards with dorgs patrolled the corridors. After the first twenty-four hours the transport began to seem like a metal prison to men who were accustomed to a life outdoors, sparring with one another and hunting in the jungle of Chthon. Fights started breaking out increasingly often, and Aton wondered if a full-scale riot might be imminent.

Aton himself spent most of his time alone in his cabin. He seldom thought of the past now. Most often, he lay on his bed imagining new kinds of torture devices and the effects they would have upon his victims. These fantasies were obsessively detailed, and occupied him for hours. In the end, though, they would madden him with sexual frustration. At such

times he would leave his cabin and head for the main
lounge, which the warriors had turned into a games
area. Here they sparred with padded swords and
wooden daggers. Alas, the pleasure of forcing one's
opponent to submit was meager and brief. Sometimes
it even seemed to make the frustration worse.

Many of the ship's walls were paneled with mirrors
to create an illusion of greater space. In the camp on
Chthon, the warriors had seldom had any opportunity
to see themselves. Here there was no way to escape the
sight of their own ruined faces.

Most of the mirrors were smashed to fragments and
ground to powder in the first day, but Aton deliberately kept the one in his cabin intact. He would stare
at his own mutilated features and feel his rage rise.
Often it would be so intense that the only way he
could release it was by taking his knife and pressing
the tip of the blade into his own flesh. The pain
blotted out his anger—and it helped him to visualize
the agony his tormentors would feel when the time
came to inflict his revenge on them.

39.

When they were just a few hours from Xerva, Oris
summoned Aton to the control room. It was a wide,
circular, low-ceilinged space with white consoles ranged
around the perimeter of a silver metal floor. Three
dorgs were sitting there, dwarfing the screens and
keyboards. Oris stood with Quentain by a six-foot
starcube. There was no one else present.

Aton looked from one of the women to the other.
Back at the camp, after his initiation, he had seldom
seen Quentain. She had now taken advantage of the
ship's supplies and had outfitted herself in a tight
white jumpsuit that clung to the shape of her body.
She wore white suede boots and platinum jewelry, like
a fashionable socialite who would make a fitting escort
for a businessman or a diplomat. As Aton dropped to
his knees before the two women, he looked at the
ample swelling of Quentain's breasts under the tight
elastic fabric. The outlines of her nipples were clearly
visible. He imagined himself stabbing, slicing, burning, and biting the soft flesh.

She saw him staring at her and straightened her
shoulders, making the fabric tighten. She gave him a
knowing, contemptuous smile, as if she understood
exactly what was in his mind, and relished his impo-
tence. One of the dorgs stood up and wandered over
to her. She patted it with one hand and shifted her
hips provocatively, as if inviting Aton to try to make a
move toward her.

Oris, meanwhile, had activated the starcube. A planet

hung in the display, turning slowly. She typed a code
on the control panel and the surface zoomed closer.
Soon the image was highly magnified, showing a small
group of buildings at the base of a range of mountains.
Aton forced himself to turn away from Quentain. He
studied the evolving 3-D images.

"This is the colony," Oris was saying. "The mountains are where the metals are: iron, aluminum, zinc,
other ores, ninety percent pure. In the valley below,
there's vegetation. That's where their food comes from.
So far as we know, almost all their equipment is automated. Right now, according to Federation data, they're
establishing intelligent systems that will be self-replicating.
You understand?" She looked at Aton as if she doubted
his ability to grasp the concept.

"They have machines building machines," he said.

She nodded. "It should be a simple matter to reprogram their production lines to produce the weapons
we need."

He looked at her doubtfully.

"We do have the capability," she told him firmly.
"Anyway, that group of buildings is where the colonists live. They have some defenses, but mainly against
local wildlife. We'll spray them with energy beams,
then send your warriors down in lifeboats. Your job is
to kill anything that lives, but don't damage any
equipment."

Aton nodded. He looked at the buildings in the
cube and imagined the people who lived there. Families full of ambition, opening up a whole new world.
Smart young men and women made beautiful by cos-
metic surgery, planning families, fulfilling all their
dreams. He hated them for everything they had that
was now denied him. It would give him grim satisfaction to educate them in the real nature of the universe:
deprivation and death.

40.

Air roared past the lifeboat hull, and it lurched sickeningly as it plummeted toward the face of the planet. There was a control panel, but it was dead. The boat was under remote command from the mother ship—the transport vehicle now in geosynchronous orbit high above.

Twenty men and twenty dorgs were squeezed into the boat. It stank of sweat. No one said anything. Everyone was watching the viewscreen. The colony buildings were growing larger: little white cubes in a field of green. They looked untouched and immaculate.

Then, as the lifeboat started decelerating to make landfall, the picture changed. A pale blue beam from the mother ship danced among the houses like a pencil-thin searchlight. Everything it touched burst into flames.

The lifeboat fell through billowing smoke. It shook and shuddered at maximum G-forces, then hit the ground.

It opened like a clamshell. Aton threw himself onto the back of his dorg, and the other warriors did the same. He shouted and pointed, but the creature already seemed to know what to do. It bounded forward. Aton clung to the harness. His sword slapped against his thigh. Smoke from the burning buildings stung his eyes.

A dozen more lifeboats were dropping out of the sky. One of them hit and burst open nearby, warriors on their dorgs pouring out like black ants. Aton felt adrenaline coursing through him. He felt excited, fright-

ened but full of lust, like a man confronted with a
virgin bride.

A woman ran out from the smoke directly in front
of his dorg. "Get her!" Aton shouted. The dog pounced,
closed its jaws around her neck, and shook her body
like a doll. Blood spouted from her carotid artery,
drenching Aton and his beast. The dorg threw her
body aside and leaped forward through the front door
into one of the colonists' homes.

Aton dismounted, afraid that as the dorg ran from
room to room he might be crushed between it and a
doorframe or a wall. The house was burning at one
side, but was otherwise intact. Aton ran into the kitchen
and found a man stumbling around, blinded by blood
running into his eyes from a cut on his forehead.
"Here," Aton shouted. He grabbed a napkin from a
table that was set for lunch, seized the man by his
shoulder, and wiped the blood away.

The man blinked at Aton. His eyes were wide with
confusion. He saw Aton's ravaged face and backed
away.

Aton grabbed the man by the front of his shirt. He
shook him angrily. "Watch me," he said. "Look in my
eyes."

He unsheathed his sword with his free hand and
jabbed it into the man's stomach. Slowly, then, he
eased it in, relishing the man's expression as he felt
himself skewered on the blade. As the colonist let out
an awful fractured scream and started vomiting blood,
Aton felt himself come. He dropped the man and
staggered back, gasping.

There was a roar from the dorg in the living room.
Aton swallowed hard and shook his head, trying to
clear it. He stumbled in the direction of the sound.

He found the dorg backed into a corner by a twelve-
year-old boy holding a hunting rifle. The kid was
shaking so hard he could barely hold the gun. It was
trained on the dorg's head, however, and the animal
obviously knew what it was. The boy clenched his jaw

and winced as if afraid of what was about to happen when he pulled the trigger.

Aton flung his dagger. It hit the boy in the neck as the gun went off. The shot blasted a hole in the ceiling, and debris rained down. The dorg leaped forward with another mighty roar and pawed the boy with its outstretched claws, ripping his clothes off and gouging his body. Aton grabbed the kid's rifle and ran outside.

He saw a ten-year-old girl running across the grass outside the house, heading for some freshly planted bushes. She was screaming and clutching a teddy bear.

Aton raised the gun and sighted on her head. Then he changed his mind and aimed lower. He pulled the trigger, and the weapon kicked hard against his shoulder. He saw the girl fall down, one of her legs blown off below the knee.

He ran forward, seized the kid, and picked her up. Her body was limp and her face was pale. She was in shock. He held her body as blood pulsed out of her thigh. He watched her, waiting for the precise moment when life would give way to death. Her eyelids flickered. The tiny muscles beside her mouth spasmed briefly. Then she was a limp, dead weight in his arms.

He dropped her body and looked around, feeling light-headed and dizzy. Buildings were still burning, but all the colonists nearby had been killed. In the distance, a couple of dorgs were chasing men who were fleeing toward the fields in the valley below. There was no cover, and the men couldn't possibly outrun their pursuers.

Screams and sounds of breaking glass came from a large factory building that stood below the foothills of the mountains that towered over the little colony. There were two gunshots, and a dorg bellowed in pain and fury. More of the animals swarmed into the building, with warriors right behind them. Moments later, four colonists were dragged out. Aton ran toward

them, but they were ripped to pieces long before he
could reach the scene.

A shadow passed across the sun. He looked up and
saw the big converted pleasure cruiser floating overhead, dropping cautiously toward a landing field at the
edge of the settlement. He realized with confusion
that the battle was already over. The colonists had
been caught entirely by surprise, and had put up
virtually no resistance. It had been a massacre.

Aton looked around him at the landscape. The mountains glowed silver, green, and yellow in the pure
white sunlight. They looked as if they had been cast
from a swirl of metals and mineral salts. Their slopes
were festooned with glittering growths of crystal, like
metallic trees. By contrast, the valley below was a rich
green-brown, its fertile soil divided into squares, each
growing a different crop. Machines were tending to
the farmland, oblivious of the slaughter that had occurred close by.

Aton sheathed his sword and wiped his bloody hands
on his breeches. This world was beautiful and rich in
every resource, but it looked tame compared with the
seething jungle of Chthon, and the battle had been
tantalizingly brief. He hoped he wouldn't have to wait
here too long. The small amount of killing he had
done made him realize how much he wanted more.

41.

Months passed. While Oris and her guards started reprogramming the automated factories and remodeling the mother ship, the warriors and their dorgs were released into the wilderness of Xerva. Out among the metal mountains and crystal trees they were free to roam—pending a time when the new weapons would be completed and the men's fighting skills would once again be in demand.

Aton lay on a high ledge overlooking a gulch layered in silver and gold. The grit under his palms looked like shards transplanted from a kaleidoscope: green chippings of copper, red iron oxides, white titanium and manganese salts, yellow chromium, blue compounds of cobalt. The rocks around him, too, were speckled with metallic hues, but the landscape had become so familiar to him that he hardly noticed the colors anymore.

His dorg lay beside him, panting in the thin air. Aton edged forward. At the bottom of the gulch was a pool of mercury that gleamed like a mirror. A twisted tree grew beside it, its branches formed from mosaics of red octahedral crystals. High in the tree sat a bird with the wingspan of an eagle and the plumage of a macaw. It preened itself, and its feathers shimmered magenta and purple in the clear white sunshine. Most creatures in the mountains were garishly pigmented. The hues were a natural result of the metal salts that they consumed in their natural diet.

Aton drew back the arrow in his homemade long-
bow, slowly, silently. He sighted down the shaft. He
had stalked this beautiful bird for most of the morning. They were rare—and thanks to him, they were
becoming rarer. The rainbow-hued tailfeathers of the
last five he had killed already ornamented his long,
matted mane of hair.

The light dimmed suddenly. The bird squawked in
surprise, flapped its great wings, and took off from its
perch. Aton glanced up and saw a circular object
hanging silently in the sky, silhouetted black against
the blue. He shaded his eyes, frowning, as the object
descended toward him.

It was large, lozenge-shaped, perhaps fifty feet in
diameter. It drifted down until it hovered over the
gulch on a level with his high vantage point. The
upper surface of its titanium hull gleamed white. It
showed no windows or external markings.

It edged toward him till it hovered close enough to
touch. A hatch hummed open. "Aton Five?" The
voice was harsh, cold, and female. Inside the vehicle
Aton saw the shadowy form of one of Oris's guards.

He sat staring at the vehicle as if unsure how to
respond. Beside him, his dorg stirred restlessly.

"Five, come aboard."

The dorg nudged Aton with its snout and gave a low
growl. Reluctantly, he stood up, shouldering his long-
bow and stowing the arrow in his quiver. He took one
last look around him at the glittering cliffs and escarp-
ments, then stepped across the metal rim of the open
hatch. The dorg followed him, and the door hummed
shut, cutting out the light.

He was led through a corridor to a circular central
control room. In the pilot's chair sat Oris, flanked by
two more dorgs and four of her guards. The walls of
the room displayed a video-synthesized panorama of
the landscape outside. Oris touched a control and the
mountain peaks dropped away as the craft lifted
smoothly and silently through the air.

Oris turned toward him. "Welcome back to civilization, Five."

The guard who had brought him in gave him a sharp
nudge, and Aton dropped down onto his knees. It had
been so long, he had almost forgotten the old reflexes.

"Traveling alone out there?" she asked.

"Yes, Oris." His voice sounded dry. Many days had
passed since he had had any need to speak.

She eyed his feathered headdress and his clothes
made from reptile skins. Their metallic scales glowed
dully in the dim interior lighting. "Not eating the
mountain wildlife, are you? I warned you and your
people three months ago about heavy-metal poisoning."

"We go down to the valley for game," he said.
"And sometimes, when we pass by the colony, we
take fruit from the fields that your machines are
cultivating."

She nodded. "I've noticed." She scanned the video
image in front of her. The landscape was drifting past,
mountain peaks flashing yellow and crimson in the
sun. An overlay of white lines appeared, plotting a
course to an X-shaped marker. "Your men are scattered all over," Oris murmured to herself.

"You said we were free to disperse—" Aton began.

"Not free," she corrected him sharply. "Never free.
I still own you, Five. I still do whatever I want with
you. You're my slave. I'm sure you remember that."

He looked down at the plastic floor in front of him.
"Yes, Oris."

Oris made a little noise of disgust. She gave a quick
signal with her hand. Aton's dorg turned toward him.
Before he had time to react, it seized his arm in its
teeth—not hard enough to puncture the skin, but hard
enough to prevent him from pulling away. "I didn't
hear what you just said, Five," she told him matter-of-
factly. "You'd better say it again."

He took a deep breath. "Yes, Oris!"

"What are you, Five?" Another hand signal, and
the dorg's jaws closed more tightly.

Aton winced as he felt the creature crushing his
arm. "I am your slave."

"I still didn't hear, Five." She made another little
hand signal. This time the creature's teeth dug deep.

Aton gasped with pain. "I am your slave!"

"Much better." She gestured, and the dorg released
him.

Aton clutched his wounded arm. He felt blood oozing where the teeth had penetrated his sleeve and
punctured his flesh beneath. He forced himself to take
deep, slow breaths. It had been a while since his rage
had been roused like this. He had never stopped dream-
ing of revenge, but it had begun to seem a slightly less
urgent obsession. The solitary life of a hunter had
been a distraction. He was glad, in a way, that Oris
had come and found him, to remind him of his need
for vengeance.

She turned back to the flier's controls. "I allowed
you and your men to spread out into the wilderness,"
she said, "because I didn't want warriors hanging around
at the colony while we were reprogramming the factories. You and your men were trained to be undisci-
plined, uncontrollable killers, not computer operators.
Now, however, it's time to bring you back. We've
produced the weapons and the vehicles we need, as
you can see for yourself." She gestured at the control
room of the ship. "It remains to be seen whether your
barbarians can be trained to use them."

The floor tilted under Aton as the flier turned, still
following its course toward the marker on the screen.
A man was down there, sitting beside a small campfire
on a rust-brown plateau. Like Aton, he was dressed in
animal skins. His ravaged face was half hidden by long
hair and an unkempt beard. His dorg sat beside him,
wearing a necklace of shrunken animal heads.

"I'm glad to see that your warriors are still in the
business of killing," said Oris. "It would have been
easier to find them, though, if they'd stayed in a
group."

"They distrust human company," said Aton. "If they had stayed in a group, they would have ended up attacking each other."

"Yes." She gave him a strange, cruel smile. "I realize that."

She turned, then, to one of her guards. "Bring in that man out there. Throw him in the cargo bay." She glanced at Aton. "You can go down there, too, Five. I've finished with you for now."

"Yes, Oris." He bowed and withdrew.

42.

They cut his beard and cropped his hair short, threw away his headdress of feathers, but let him keep his clothes fashioned from metallic hide. The clothes were warm, light, and tough; they were good body armor, and they had the primitive look that Oris seemed to think was appropriate for a warrior.

Back at the colony, Aton decided to move into the ruined home of the family he had massacred. Half of it had burned to the ground, and the remaining half still smelled of soot and wood smoke. The kitchen was a shambles, its walls and floor stained with enormous dark blotches of blood. He would sit there with his dorg each morning, eating packs of bland processed food that came from the fields in the valley, while he sharpened his hunting knife and remembered the look in the eyes of the man he had skewered with his sword.

During the daytime, he and his men were put to work learning the new military hardware. They were supplied with hand-held heat guns that would fry an enemy regardless of any armor he was wearing. They were taught to drive all-terrain personnel carriers armed with particle-beam weapons, with room inside for four warriors and their dorgs. They were not allowed to control fliers of the type that Oris had been piloting, however. These were reserved exclusively for the women.

The colony had been fortified during the past three months. Oris and her guards had moved into the fac-

tory buildings, which were now shielded with defense
fields that would repel anything from a bullet to a
high-powered beam weapon. The women were thus
protected not only from offworld forces, but from the
warriors who camped in the land around them.

It was now four weeks since his return to the colony, and his training was almost complete. For the last
few days, Oris had paired Aton with Peck, the tall,
blond, handsome man whose cheek he had defaced
with the marking stone. Peck was one of the few
warriors whom Aton genuinely feared. The man was
seemingly easygoing, seemingly relaxed; he didn't pick
fights and he didn't make trouble. His eyes seemed to
miss nothing, though, and his violent impulses might
even be comparable to Aton's own.

Clearly, Oris had an ulterior motive for pairing them.
He guessed she might be testing his authority as commander of the warriors, since Peck was one of the few
who might be strong enough, physically and mentally,
to threaten him. Alternatively, it might simply be an
idle pleasure for her to put men together who were
most likely to clash.

Aton was up at dawn. It was his habit, these days,
to work at a little bench he had set up in the bedroom
on top of what had once been a dressing table. Cos-
metics and jewelry lay in a heap on the floor where
he'd dumped them three weeks previously. A vise had
been bolted into the wood, and he had acquired an
old-fashioned power hacksaw, metal files, taps and
dies, and a drill press.

He was screwing a new three-inch length of square-
sectioned steel bar into the vise when he saw Peck
walking across the grass toward the house, a dorg
pacing along beside him. Aton paused and watched
the man. He and his animal both moved with the same
hunter's poise.

Peck disappeared from view. A moment later, he
was knocking on the door downstairs. "Five?"

Aton's dorg, lying on the bedroom floor, growled

and turned its head in the direction of the sound. Aton said nothing.

He heard Peck's footsteps on the stairs, and the clicking of dorg claws. Peck paused in the doorway. "Ready when you are, Five." His pale eyes moved quickly, taking in the room.

"One minute." Aton switched on the power saw and made a diagonal cut down the side of the steel bar. He loosened the vise, rotated the bar, tightened the vise, and made a second cut. He repeated the process twice more, creating a four-sided spike.

"What's that?" said Peck, as Aton switched off the saw and its noise died away.

He clamped the spike, drilled into one end of it, threaded the hole he had made, then picked up his armor of metal-hide. A large area down the front of it had been embellished with a profusion of metal points and blades. Aton placed the newly-cut spike among the rest, and guided a retaining screw into the base of it from the back of the cloth. He tightened the screw carefully, then held the assemblage up, checking his handiwork.

"Not bad," said Peck. He attempted to grin but some of his facial muscles had been severed during his initiation, and the best he could manage, now, was an ugly grimace.

Aton thrust his arms through two holes in the armor and pulled it on. It covered his chest and hips, and fastened at the rear. The metal spikes and serrated knife blades bristled like erect porcupine quills, confronting any attacker who might face him.

"Should stop anyone getting too close," said Peck.

"Yes," Aton said calmly, "it should." He removed the armor and laid it aside, then turned and walked to the bed. His sword was there, thrust into the mattress up to its hilt. Sometimes during the night, in fits of rage, he would slash and stab at the bed, imagining the couple who had once slept in it. He himself always slept on the floor.

Aton seized the handle of the sword, pulled it out of the bed, and sheathed it.

Peck shook his head. "You won't need that. I got your heat gun back from the shop." He handed the weapon to Aton in its holster.

Aton weighed it in his hand, checked it, and buckled it around his waist. He didn't discard the sword, however. He adjusted it so that its handle easily cleared the heat gun's grip, then strode across the room, walked past Peck, and started down the stairs.

One of the all-terrain personnel carriers was parked in what had once been a small flower garden at the front of the house. The carrier's cleated metal tracks had reduced the area to a mess of churned mud.

"Anything new today?" said Peck, as he followed Aton out of the house and climbed into the vehicle.

"Exercises. Like yesterday." Aton waited for the two dorgs to get in, then closed the hatch and started the carrier's power unit. He disliked sharing its small interior. Peck's style was low-key, but he had an intensity that was hard to ignore.

Aton activated the energy shield, then engaged the drive and moved the vehicle forward. He took a long, curving path across what had once been a landscaped area dotted with colonists' homes. The armored vehicle mashed flowers into the mud. Its wedge-shaped front end uprooted bushes and severed small trees. There was the distant sound of splintering wood, and debris scraped under the carrier's belly. The rear viewscreen showed a swathe of destruction carved across the landscape.

The main factory buildings came into view on the right, moving slowly past. "There they are," said Peck. "Armed and protected. Safe and sound."

Aton didn't bother to answer.

"No home-defense screens for us," said Peck. "But then, we're expendable, isn't that right?"

Aton gave him a cold, steady stare. "You should check your scope," he said.

Peck nodded slowly. "Yes, sir." His tone was sardonic. He switched on the target-finder in front of him and peered into the eyepiece. "Nothing," he said. He sat back and glanced up at the rear viewscreen as the factory buildings receded behind the carrier. "Something I've wondered, Five, is why the colonists who were here before didn't put in defenses the way we've done."

Aton guided the vehicle up the first of the foothills at the base of the metal mountains. To his left he saw robot mining equipment at work, carving ores out of the ground. "Piracy is a small risk," he said. "The galaxy is full of planets that haven't been developed yet. There's wealth for everyone. And they were probably intending to arm themselves once their factory became operational." He stopped speaking abruptly, realizing that Peck had prompted him to talk more than he intended.

"Lucky, wasn't it, hitting this place when we did," said Peck. "Just when they got their gear set up, but not so far along that they were able to put up a fight."

Aton glanced across at him. "Lucky?"

Peck shrugged. "Either that, or the women had access to some very good intelligence. And a whole lot of knowledge about reprogramming manufacturing equipment."

"What are you getting at?" said Aton. He reduced speed as the carrier approached the summit of the hill.

"Nothing." Peck's expression was unreadable.

"Scope," Aton reminded him.

He peered into the finder. "Still no sign. Maybe the next hill over."

"And maybe not." Aton turned the vehicle, detouring around the summit.

For a while there was silence in the cabin, broken only by the whine of the carrier's motors and the rumble of its tracks across the hard terrain.

"You know," Peck said after a minute, "I've heard

some of the men talking about what we should do now we've got the weapons."

"Talking?" Aton kept his eyes on the terrain.

"I figured maybe you already knew about it, seeing that you're the commander. I've heard men say that we could have this planet all to ourselves. Without anyone telling us what to do."

Aton brought the personnel carrier to a slow halt. He turned and looked hard at Peck. "Are you really suggesting we could wipe out all the women, and the dorgs?"

Peck's eyes stared steadily back. "I'm not suggesting anything, friend. Just telling you what I've heard."

Aton said nothing.

"Of course," Peck went on, "if it happened, a lot of men would be wondering whose side you'd be on."

"My own," Aton said without hesitation. He upped the carrier's power and moved it forward again, edging around a mesa of layered zinc and copper ores. A tiny point of light caught his attention, high on a ridge at the opposite side of a valley just ahead. "Check that," he said.

Peck peered into the target finder. "Ah, yes. Target in view." He adjusted controls beside the finder. "Looks like Wingrove's carrier."

Aton switched to reverse gear. He edged back behind the mesa. "They see us?"

There was a muffled explosion from outside the vehicle. Part of the mesa vaporized, spitting fragments of metal ore. "Seems to me they did," said Peck.

"Hit them." Aton's fist clenched reflexively. The carriers were shielded, of course, so that no damage could be done with these war games, which were nothing more than harmless target practice. At the same time, he liked to imagine the particle beam melting the opposing vehicle and frying the men inside it.

"Lining up." Peck made quick hand movements. "They're taking evasive action, but—" He pressed the fire button. "Hit."

"Good," Aton said quietly. He engaged forward gear and took his own vehicle out from the shadow of the mesa. It moved a few feet, then shuddered. A grinding sound came from the left side. Quickly, he disengaged power.

"Sounds like a cleat bolt," said Peck.

Aton nodded. He paused. He didn't like working with machinery; at the same time, he didn't trust Peck to do the job. "I'll have to go out there. Announce it." He waited, watching Peck.

The man picked up a communications unit and thumbed the transmit button. "All units, this is Unit One. We're dropping our shield. Repeat, dropping our shield. Making repairs. Confirm."

Aton waited while the other units called back their confirmations one by one. Then he powered down the defense field and opened the hatch.

Chunks of ore lay scattered on the ground, still semimolten from the other vehicle's beam attack. The air smelled metallic. Aton glanced around, feeling vulnerable. Still, with the shield down, Peck was equally undefended. The thin metal shell of the carrier provided no beam protection.

Aton inspected the left track and found that one of the bolts that linked the cleats had worked halfway out and was scraping the body of the vehicle. He searched around, found a small rock, and started hammering the bolt back into place.

"Tool kit?" Peck called from inside the vehicle.

"No," said Aton.

"We don't want it to work loose again. Maybe you can bend the end of the bolt over, or flatten it."

Aton inspected the part. It was hard to see why its head had fractured off.

"You could use your heat gun," Peck suggested. "That ought to soften it enough for you to mash it."

"All right." Aton drew the weapon—then paused with his finger on the trigger. He waited a long moment.

"Is it working?" Peck called. His voice sounded tense; wrong, somehow.

Aton holstered the weapon. "No. I changed my mind." He climbed back into the carrier and slammed the hatch behind him. He revved the motor and turned back toward the colony.

"What are you doing?" Peck looked surprised and unsure of himself.

"Taking it back for proper repairs," said Aton. "The bolt took this long to work loose, it'll last the same distance back to base."

"We'll lose our score," Peck pointed out.

Aton didn't bother to answer. Unobtrusively, he dropped one hand to the hilt of his sword, keeping his other on the steering lever.

Peck eyed him warily for a moment, then shrugged and sat back in his seat, folding his arms.

43.

There were a dozen guards and as many dorgs waiting when the carrier reached the main entrance to the factory buildings. "Leave your vehicle," an amplified voice told them. "Get out and stand beside it. Do not make any sudden movements."

Peck looked questioningly at Aton. "What—"

"We'd better do what they say." Aton swung out of the vehicle into the sunlight. His dorg joined him, its ears pricked up, its eyes alert.

Peck and his dorg climbed down to the ground. A dozen guards ran out from the main gate and seized him. His weapon was taken. Handcuffs were slapped on his wrists. The last Aton saw of his face, his eyes were wide with surprise. He shouted protests as they dragged him away.

"Oris wants to see you," another of the guards said to Aton. She took his sword and heat gun. "Come this way."

He was led through corridors he'd never been allowed to enter before. Finally, at the door to her room, his guide passed his weapons to one of Oris's honor guards, and he was admitted.

It was a large, bare space with a stainless-steel floor and a white desk at the center. Screens on the walls showed views of the factory complex: snaking conduits, catwalks, ducts, machine tools ranged in rows. Almost all the production lines seemed to have been shut down.

She stood behind her desk. He kneeled. "Did you

realize my people were monitoring your conversation with Peck?" she asked without preliminaries.

Aton paused. "That hadn't occurred to me," he said.

"We do it routinely. The technology here makes it easy enough." She examined him skeptically. "Did you know before about the rebellion he was planning?"

"No."

"You hadn't heard any of this talk he referred to?"

"Most of the men are scared of me. Like Peck, they aren't sure whose side I'm on. I prefer it that way. They leave me alone."

She threw herself back into her chair and folded her arms, giving him a brooding look. "You're too smart for your own good, Five, that's what I don't like about you. Peck, I knew from the start what he was planning. I paired him with you to see which way you'd go." She drummed her fingers on the desk. "What happened out there, anyway?"

"I think he tried to kill me. When he told me to use my heat gun on the cleat bolt—it sounded wrong."

"Take Five's weapon down the hall and have it inspected," Oris snapped to one of her guards. She waited while the woman left the room. "Not that it makes much difference," she went on. "He'll be tortured to death tonight anyway, as a message to the men who were stupid enough to take his ideas seriously. And tomorrow, we're gone."

Aton knew better than to ask a question. He waited in silence, keeping his expression, as always, carefully neutral.

"We're ready," Oris explained. "Our battleground's been chosen. A planet named Minion."

This time Aton was not quite able to conceal his reaction. He tensed as he heard the name. He felt a nervous tic pull at his cheek.

She smiled faintly. "The name means something to you."

"Yes, Oris," he said through the tightness in his chest.

"I know it does, Five. Your escape from Hvee, with your Minion bride, is in Federation records. She was the one who abandoned you on Chthon—is that right?"

"Yes, Oris." Again he felt his muscles tug at him in little spasms.

Her strong, cruel mouth widened fractionally. "So do you have sentimental attachment to Minion? Is it going to bother you when we go in there and burn it down?"

Aton remembered the cloned Minionettes—replicas of Malice, every one. He saw himself slaughtering them, incinerating them with his heat gun, delicately slicing their pure white skin with his sword. "It will be a privilege," he said slowly.

Oris laughed shortly. "Sometimes I think we did the job too well on you, Five. All right, our plan is to spend just a few hours inflicting as much damage as we can. It's a Proscribed world, so they have no trade, therefore no technology, therefore no firepower, which makes our job that much easier. We'll move on before the Federation has time to respond." She clasped her hands in front of her. "Are you wondering why we're fighting this battle?"

In fact, the thought hadn't occurred to him. He had come to see bloodshed as an end in itself.

She shrugged. "It's none of your business. I'll tell you, though, you and your warriors can look forward to a lot of killing. There'll be a whole series of hit-and-run attacks. I'm sure that makes you happy."

He wondered, briefly, if anything would actually make him happy. Happiness was something he hadn't thought about at all in the past months. Avenging himself on his enemies would give him satisfaction, when the time came; but he doubted he would ever feel actual happiness again.

The guard returned with his weapon disassembled in

her hands. "The coil has been reversed, Oris." She laid it on the desk and stepped back.

She looked at it sharply, then back at Aton. "You put this in for repairs?"

"Yes, Oris." Aton said.

"If you'd used this weapon, the beam would have been inverted. It would have fried you instantly. Peck would probably have blamed it on a mistake in the repair shop."

Aton felt a spasm of overwhelming rage—this time not at Oris but at Peck, for trying to kill him.

44.

That evening the warriors gathered to watch Peck's execution. He was tied to a tall metal strut driven into the ground outside the factory buildings, much as Garvin had been tied to a stake in the compound back on Chthon. His naked body still looked impressively powerful, even with his arms stretched up above his head. His tanned skin was mottled with bruises where the guards had routinely beaten him, and his mouth was bloody. He breathed in short, painful gasps. His pale blue eyes stared straight ahead, as if he were focusing on some source of strength that only he could see.

"Some of you know what this scum was hoping to do," Oris addressed the men. "He actually thought he had a chance to rebel against us." She grinned humorlessly, turning slowly, scrutinizing each man in turn.

Peck still stared straight ahead. His legs, though, were starting to tremble. Aton wondered, with detachment, how he must feel, knowing he was about to be tortured slowly to death.

"This scum," Oris went on calmly, "thought he could organize you. Some of you believed him. I know who you are." Again, she slowly scanned the crowd. "I monitored your conversations. Nothing will happen to you at this time. Remember, though, I know your names, and I know what you said. I can do the same thing to you that I'm going to do to Peck here, if you show the slightest sign of disloyalty."

Aton glanced at the warriors in the crowd. Some

seemed nervous. He carefully noted which ones they were.

"All right, start killing him," Oris said. She turned and walked away.

Quentain stepped forward. Aton hadn't seen her in the past three months, but she was exactly the way he remembered her. The nubile body was tightly wrapped in a lavender-blue jumpsuit. The long blond hair caught the mellow rays of the sunset as she looked Peck slowly up and down like an artist examining a blank canvas. A guard brought forward a tray of tools, and Aton remembered, with a pang of instinctive fear, the primitive implements she'd used on him when he'd been strapped on her operating table. The tools she had at her disposal now, however, looked technologically sophisticated.

"Lights," she said. Floodlights came to life, bathing the area. Peck squinted into the glare.

Quentain picked up a small metal cylinder and thumbed a switch. A bright yellow triangle, like a tightly focused lightbeam, sprang from one end. "This is an industrial cutting tool," she explained to Peck. "We use it to shape high-carbon steel." She watched him intently with her clear blue eyes. She was no longer an artist; she was a sadistic child with a magnifying glass, preparing to roast ants one by one and watch them wriggle as they died.

Peck closed his eyes. He started shaking uncontrollably. He lost control of his bowels, and the smell of his shit drifted on the warm evening air.

Quentain used the tool to carve a one-inch chunk out of his heavily muscled thigh. The plasma blade cauterized the wound as it cut the flesh, so there was no blood—only pain.

The warriors stared in brooding silence as Peck screamed and struggled. The warriors' eyes were intense and unblinking. Many of them were beginning to breathe heavily.

Quentain set aside her blade for a moment and

picked up a bottle of acid. She squirted some into Peck's left eye.

Aton turned away. Discreetly, he left the crowd. He felt angry and frustrated—angry that Peck wasn't suffering more, and frustrated that he wasn't the torturer. He, after all, had been Peck's intended victim. The least he deserved was a chance to take revenge in his own fashion. The way Quentain was going about things, Peck would be dead in a matter of hours. If Aton had his way, it would take weeks.

Back at his makeshift home, he heated a food pack and carried it up to the bedroom so that he could work while he ate. He unrolled the leather apron and carefully laid out his tools. As darkness gathered outside the windows, and Peck's screams of agony sounded faintly in the distance, Aton started sharpening each pyramid-shaped four-inch steel spike to a pinpoint and mounting them carefully in the body armor.

Now that he knew that the battle was to be fought on Minion, it was all the more important to finish this little construction project ahead of time.

45.

It was claustrophobic in the personnel carrier. The air stank of animals and flesh. Four warriors were strapped into their seats, with four dorgs crammed into a small padded area at the back. Aton's armor was heavy across his chest. He shifted uncomfortably, feeling himself sweating under it.

All the viewscreens were blank, because the vehicle was sealed inside the dark cargo bay of a flier, with seven other personnel carriers. The flier, in turn, was stowed with five others like it inside the mother ship, whose luxury amenities for interstellar travelers had been ripped out during renovations on Xerva. Its sole purpose now was to transport the warriors in their killing machines from one world to another.

Gravity seemed to shift, and the floor turned. "Orbital injection," said a voice from a loudspeaker in Aton's communication unit. "We are now orbiting planet Minion."

He tried to visualize the landscape of simple little villages two hundred miles below. Beautiful verdant country, primitive wooden dwellings. He'd been there less than a standard year ago, but in his imagination it now seemed as unreal as a scene from an entertainment tape.

"What's taking so long?" complained the warrior sitting beside him. His name was Rovin; he was a big, bearded bear of a man with a shaven head and a steel-mesh waistcoat that hung open to expose his chest. Metal rings had been set in his ears, nose, and nipples.

"They have to get into the right position before we can drop," Aton said. "There's a whole planet down there. Some parts aren't even inhabited."

Rovin took his knife from its sheath, ran his thumb along its blade, then restlessly stowed it again. "Still seems to me we been waiting long enough. I want to get me one of them Minion women. The way I hear it—"

He broke off with a grunt as the carrier seemed to fall from under them. For a moment they were completely weightless. "Fliers released," said the voice over the loudspeaker. "Five minutes to landfall."

Aton rehearsed it in his head. The flier would hit the ground. The doors of its cargo bay would open. He'd up the power and take the personnel carrier roaring out onto the planet's surface. After that, search and destroy; kill and burn.

His seat swayed and rocked as the flier carrying them fell through pockets of air turbulence. One of the dorgs made an unhappy whining noise, and the warrior sitting behind Aton suddenly threw up. His vomit spattered onto the steel floor, and the smell of it quickly spread through the vehicle. No one said anything now; they were tense and ready, watching the viewscreens.

More air turbulence. Then severe G-forces. Finally, the thud of contact.

The screens lit up as the cargo doors opened. Daylight flooded in. Aton took the carrier down a steel ramp and out onto a field of tall grass and wild blossoms. A line of blue-gray trees was close by; beyond them, a cultivated field. The crop looked like barley, rippling in the wind. A peasant holding a scythe was staring open-mouthed at the silvery ovoid of the flier with tracked vehicles swarming out of it.

"Kill him," Aton told Rovin.

The big man did target acquisition and pressed the

fire button. The farmer burst into flames, along with a large area of his field and the trees that bordered it. Rovin grinned. "Yeah!" he whooped. "All right!"

"Turn ninety right, Unit One," said the voice over the comm unit. "You'll come to a dirt road. Proceed left to the first village."

Aton acknowledged and followed the directions. He saw the other personnel carriers fanning out in different directions. In the distance, beyond the row of flaming trees, was a wooden castle at the top of a low hill. Aton recognized it: the so-called palace of the self-styled King of Minion. Aton remembered his night as a prisoner there, when he'd come to Minion with Malice and his offworld status had been discovered. He remembered the humiliation of being trapped in a stinking jail cell with straw on the floor. Too bad his orders were now taking him in the opposite direction; he'd enjoy burning that building to the ground.

As if in answer to his wishes, a pale blue beam flickered from above and danced briefly across the hilltop. The palace exploded in a fireball. Moments later, the personnel carrier rocked as the pressure wave hit it.

He turned the vehicle onto the dirt road. A horse and cart were just ahead. The driver was a typical Minion man: scrawny, bearded, with a mean, ugly little face. His beautiful red-haired wife sat behind him, demurely veiled.

Aton glanced at Rovin. "What are you waiting for?"

"Looking, that's all. Figuring maybe to blow off that veil without taking her face with it." He fumbled with his controls.

The driver of the cart saw the personnel carrier coming at him and stood up, preparing to jump for the ditch. Rovin hit the fire button. The blast from the beam blew the Minion man's head, arms, and legs off and sent his torso spiraling away, spraying blood like a decapitated lawn sprinkler. The animal that had been pulling the cart exploded. The cart itself was turned on

its side, throwing the woman onto the ground. She lay
there unconscious, oozing blood.

Aton accelerated. The carrier's tracks bumped over
her, mashing her body into the mud.

The village was visible at the top of the next hill.
Tiny figures were running across the fields, fleeing as
the vehicle approached. "Pick them off," said Aton.

"All right, all right, man, I'm taking care of it."
Rovin tapped the fire button, and one by one the
running figures popped like balloons in a shooting
gallery, leaving splashes of pink and red on the green
fields.

"Want me to do the village?" said Rovin.

"Yes, but use minimum power. People could be
hiding in cellars. We don't want to bury them. That'd
make it harder to get them out and kill them."

"Gotcha." Rovin made adjustments. As the carrier
rumbled into the village street, he swung the beam
down one line of houses, then another, blasting their
walls aside in a flurry of planks and beams.

Aton stopped the carrier in a little square at the
center of the village. "Time out," he said. "Ten minutes, no more, understood?" He opened the hatch.

In truth, the whole job could have been taken care
of from inside the carrier; but he wanted personal
contact, and he knew the other warriors wanted it too.

Small fires were crackling all around. Smoke was
billowing up into the sky. Women were screaming.
Animals were running wildly to and fro.

Aton was high on adrenaline and blood lust. He
hardly felt the weight of his spiked metal armor. He
ran toward a heap of timbers that had once been an
inn, and drew his heat gun. A man was climbing out
from the debris with blood running from a scalp wound.
"Hey," said Aton.

The man looked up, startled. Aton shot him in the
face with a minimum charge—just enough to burn the
skin off, set his hair on fire, and burst his eyeballs.
The man tumbled backward, blood choking his screams.

Another man was emerging. He seemed virtually unhurt. He looked at his screaming companion, saw Aton, and drew his sword.

Aton played the gun briefly over the blade, heating it till it glowed red. The man dropped it with a yell as the heat reached the handle and seared his hand.

Aton switched the gun's beam briefly to the man's crotch, setting his trousers on fire and burning his genitals off. But he was already losing interest. "Kill," he said, and pointed. His dorg loped forward, fell on the writhing body, and quickly ripped it to pieces.

Aton glanced around. His three companions were working their way around the square, incinerating every man, woman, child, and animal they encountered. Aton watched for a moment. The wholesale butchery stirred him briefly; but he needed more.

He ran past flaming huts and cabins to one that was still basically intact. A peasant was standing in the doorway, peering out, pale with fear. He tried to slam the door as Aton approached, but wasn't quick enough. Aton hot-beamed the peasant's legs, and he fell down screaming.

Aton stepped over him and found himself in a tiny dirt-floored room. A woman was cowering in one corner. Aton stared at her for a moment, confused by her exact resemblance to Malice. Then he felt his rage rise up. "Out," he shouted at her, and gestured with his gun.

She'd seen what the weapon had done to her husband. She obeyed quickly and silently, sliding around the edge of the room with her back to the wall, till she reached the little doorway. "Into the street," Aton snapped at her. She backed away, stepping over her husband lying writhing in agony.

"Does his pain make you feel good?" Aton asked, following the woman into the street. "Does it? Or how about the way I feel?"

She stared at him blankly, her face deathly pale and her chest heaving.

"Come on, woman!" he shouted at her. "Tell me!"

"I—feel dizzy," she gasped, as if the onslaught of emotions was overloading her telepathic sensitivity.

"Leave her alone," her husband shouted from behind Aton. He started dragging himself out into the street on his belly, trailing his ruined legs behind him.

Aton turned, aimed carefully, and burned the man's fingers off.

The woman screamed in rage and seized Aton from behind, where he was relatively unprotected by his armor. Her fingers curled around his head and ripped at his face. Then she grabbed his gun arm and tried to sink her teeth into it. She was a bundle of fury, red hair swirling, hands clutching feverishly.

Aton's dorg bounded forward. It bit into the woman's legs. Its massive jaws closed with full force, crunching her bones as it pulled her away from him.

Aton realized he had forgotten the strength and ferocity of Minionettes. He cursed his own complacency. "Let her go," he told the dorg.

Obediently, the creature backed off. The red-haired woman lay in the dirt, bleeding profusely. "I'm going to make you wish you'd never tried to hurt me," Aton told her. He uncoiled the rope that he carried at his hip, fashioned a noose, and slipped it over her head. He tied the other end around the shoulders of his dorg. "Take her to the carrier," he said, pointing.

The dorg loped across the cobblestones, hauling the woman behind it. Aton followed, enjoying her throttled cries as she clutched at the rope around her neck while her bloody legs trailed in the dirt.

The men were assembling with their dorgs back at the vehicle. One warrior was holding two severed heads like a couple of bagged bowling balls. Another was feeding a baby's arm to his dorg.

"Unit One," the loudspeaker inside the vehicle was complaining. "Acknowledge, Unit One."

Aton ignored it. He untied the rope from the dorg and tied it instead to a bar at the rear of the personnel

carrier. The woman was still struggling to free herself
from the noose around her neck, but her struggles
were futile. The knot had pulled tight.

"Okay, inside," said Aton.

The men and their dorgs piled into their vehicle.
The men were breathing heavily. None of them said
anything, but their faces were flushed and they shared
the same look of furtive, private satisfaction.

Aton reached to close the hatch—then stopped as
he saw a man on a horse galloping into the village
square. One of the king's army, he realized. The man
wore chain-mail armor and a metal helmet. He had
drawn his sword and was brandishing it, screaming a
battle cry.

Aton aimed carefully at the man's helmet and fired
a medium burst from his heat gun. The helmet glowed
red-hot.

The man shouted in pain and fell off his horse. He
scrabbled around on the ground, trying to undo the
strap that secured his helmet to his head. He was so
crazed with pain he couldn't loosen the buckle.

Aton reset the gun to its lowest setting, then played
it on the helmet some more, literally broiling the man's
brains. The body started twitching and thrashing. His
back arched, he went rigid, then flopped over.

Aton smiled to himself, slammed the hatch, and
returned to his seat in the personnel carrier. "Unit
One reporting," he said, as he started out of the
square.

"Five, did you abandon your vehicle?"

"We had to take care of some stuff outside, in
person."

There was a short silence. "You will explain when
you return. Burn this village and proceed to the next."

He nodded to Rovin. The beefy man upped the
intensity of the personnel carrier's particle beam and
swept it around. The whole village exploded into flame
as the vehicle moved out and into the open country
beyond.

Aton checked the rear viewscreen. The Minionette was still being dragged behind the personnel carrier by the rope around her neck. Her body was being pummeled and thrown from side to side by ruts and stones in the road. Her chewed legs were leaving a trail of blood.

The sight gave Aton some satisfaction. But he needed more.

46.

He stopped the vehicle when they were halfway to the next village. He sat in his seat, silently staring at the screens showing the landscape outside.

"What's up?" Rovin asked.

Aton turned toward him. "Take over."

"What?" Rovin stared at him. So did the two warriors sitting behind.

Aton pulled himself out of his seat, moving awkwardly in his heavy armor. "I have something to do out there. Pick me up on your way back."

Rovin glanced at the other men, then back at Aton. "You crazy? This ain't what Oris—"

"Just do it," Aton said. "It's my responsibility."

Rovin shrugged. "Okay, boss." He slid across to the controls.

As Aton opened the hatch and stepped out, he heard a warning growl from his dorg. It pushed quickly forward between the warriors and the other dorgs. Its teeth were bared, its eyes glaring yellow.

Aton grabbed the top edge of the open hatch, braced himself, then managed to haul himself up onto the roof of the vehicle. The dorg saw him, twisted around, and started climbing up after him. Its claws scrabbled ineffectually across the armor plate.

Aton drew his gun and fired at the animal's head. It fell backward onto the ground and started making horrible coughing sounds. Its black body writhed and its skin rippled. Its head was mostly burned off, reduced to a scorched stump.

"Jesus Christ, Five, you're dead!" one of the warriors shouted.

Aton slammed the hatch shut. He didn't want any of the other dorgs to come out after him. He turned and methodically burned his own dorg with his gun until its flesh was reduced to ash.

He turned back toward the vehicle. He knew that the warriors inside were watching him on the viewscreens. "Go," he said pointing on down the track. "I know what I'm doing."

After a moment the vehicle's power unit whined and it rumbled away, bumping along the rutted road, still dragging the body of the Minionette behind it. He noticed, without much interest, that she now seemed to be dead.

Aton paused a moment, breathing deeply, as if preparing himself for what lay ahead. Then he vaulted a gate and ran from the dirt road through a field of tall grass. He tried to figure the most likely sequence of events. Oris and her guards would be monitoring all the forty-eight personnel carriers and their warriors. Discipline would be breaking down everywhere, with men stopping and killing at random. Chances were that Aton's brief command to Rovin to take over the controls of the carrier wouldn't have been noticed. And the warriors in his unit probably wouldn't report what he'd done to his dorg—at least, not right away. They'd be too confused and afraid of some sort of reprisal for letting it happen. So he had a good chance of being left alone for at least an hour, maybe more.

He had recognized the landscape, with a terrible sinking sensation, as the vehicle passed between the hedgerows on the narrow dirt road. Less than a year ago, but a lifetime away, he had followed Malice along this road. Her little cabin was not far from here. He increased his pace. He dreaded seeing it—but he knew he had to.

When the cabin came into view among the trees it was just as he remembered it. He stopped and stood for a moment, breathing hard. A wisp of smoke came from the little building's chimney. Someone, evidently, was home.

Aton circled around, trying to stay out of sight among the trees. He reached a point opposite the cabin's front door, crouched down, and aimed his heat gun. He remembered the first evening when she had brought him here: his terrible indecision, his guilt, his lust for her that finally swept his inhibitions aside. At that time, he had only known her identity as his mother for a matter of days. He had still been trying to come to terms with it. Meanwhile, she had seduced him as she always did, playing on his obsession with her, goading him, provoking his sadism and then feeding off it.

He aimed at the door and fired a quick burst, using a tight beam so that only the door itself caught fire.

There were shouts from inside the cabin. A scrawny Minion man kicked the door open, then knocked the flaming timbers to the ground. A woman appeared holding a bucket of water. She threw it over the flames.

Aton emerged from his hiding place. "Get inside," he shouted, brandishing the heat gun. "Or I'll burn you both, just as I did the door."

They looked at each other, then started backing away from him, into the little building. He followed them and paused in the doorway.

The green-eyed, red-haired woman was reaching for a kitchen knife. She looked scared but proud as she grabbed it and held the blade high. The man, meanwhile, had drawn his sword. "Who are you?" he challenged Aton. "What do you want here, offworlder?"

Aton aimed his heat gun, taking care that the beam wouldn't touch the wooden wall and set the rest of the cabin on fire. He let the man have a short burst in his stomach.

He dropped his sword and clutched himself, howling as the contents of his stomach boiled inside him. Aton calmly picked up the sword, grabbed the man by his hair, and dragged him outside. The woman, mean-while, stood staring in horror.

"Stop," he warned her, as she started coming after him with the kitchen knife. He raised the sword warningly. "Get back in there."

She hesitated, eyed the spikes and blades of his armor, then stepped backward. Her face was full of panic and confusion. "Why?" she cried out. "Why are you doing this?"

Aton dumped the man on the ground, rolled him onto his back, raised the sword, and jammed it down. The blade skewered his belly and sank into the soil beneath, pinning him like a beetle in a display case. Blood started bubbling out of the wound. He waved his arms and legs feebly, coughed, twitched, and died.

"Put down the knife," Aton warned the woman as he walked back toward the cabin. "Or I'll kill you too."

She dropped the blade. "Why?" she demanded again.

He stood in the doorway. "Get on the bed," he told her.

She stared at him, sensing the wild emotions in his mind. She edged a little way toward the bed in the corner of the room, then stopped, reluctant to go further.

He drew his own sword. "Damn you, do what I say!" He jabbed her quickly with the tip, drawing blood.

She cried out and slumped backward onto the simple mattress. "Don't!"

"Lie on your back," he ordered her. "Spread your arms and legs."

Slowly, fearfully, she did as he said.

Aton picked up a rough towel hanging beside a wash bowl by the window. He quickly sliced it into four strips with his sword, then walked to the woman and started using them to tie her wrists and ankles to each corner of the bedframe. He took savage pleasure in pulling the knots tight, watching the fabric cut into

her pure white skin. Then he stepped back and surveyed her.

"Tell me your name," he said.

"Grief," she answered. Her breasts rose and fell
quickly under her thin cotton dress. "My name is
Grief."

He sat down on the edge of the bed and shook his
head, rejecting her answer. "Your name is Malice."

"No." The woman sounded confused. "Malice is my
cousin."

"You're lying. This is Malice's cabin."

The woman squirmed on the bed. "Yes, yes, it's her
cabin. But I moved here after she—after she left Minion." She tossed her head from side to side as if trying
to clear it. "What are you *doing*? Why did you—" A
sob caught in her throat. "Why did you kill my
husband?"

"No. He wasn't your husband. I'm your husband."
Aton stood up.

"But I've never seen you before!"

"You're lying. I recognize you. Your name is Malice."

She drew a breath and screamed as loudly as she
could. The sound was deafening in the little room.

"There's no one within a mile," he told her quietly.
"This cabin is totally isolated. That's why you chose it,
Malice, remember?" He bent over her, grabbed the
hem of her dress, cut it with his dagger, then ripped it
up the front, exposing the full length of her body.

"What do you want?" she asked, wide-eyed and
pleading.

"This is what I want." He climbed onto the bed and
lowered himself onto her—slowly, tentatively, so that
the spikes protruding from the front of his armor just
barely pricked her body. He held himself in that position, breathing heavily, while he watched her face.

She tugged frantically at the bonds securing her to
the bed. They were tight. She tried to shrink into the
mattress beneath. It was firm. He lowered himself a

208

fraction farther, and the spikes dug deeper into her
soft white skin. She screamed in pain and horror.

"But Malice, you always like it when I hurt you,"
he told her. "You get excited, making me mad and
having me take it out on you." He grabbed her red
hair and jerked her head to face him. "Damn you,
isn't that right?"

"It wasn't me!" she moaned.

"Look in my head and feel the way I feel right
now," he told her. "Isn't that good? Feel how cruel I
am. Doesn't that make you excited? Eh?" He gave his
wrist a savage twist, tightening his grip on her hair.

"Too much." She winced as if trying to block out
his emotions. Tears started running down her cheeks.
"It's too much. It hurts. Please, leave me alone!"

He lowered himself an inch, letting his weight drive
the spikes into her.

She screamed and started sobbing.

"Beg for mercy," he told her.

"I beg you!"

Brutally, he dropped his full weight onto her. "You
showed me no mercy when you abandoned me on
Chthon. Why should I show you any?" Her face was
just inches from his. He watched her expression, enjoying her pain. A Minionette's body had the power to
resist injury and heal itself—within limits. He knew he
was now exceeding those limits.

"Please," she begged again. She looked up at him
imploringly.

He slid his hands behind her back, till his arms were
wrapped around her. He locked his fingers together,
then started hugging her to him, pulling her harder
and harder against him. The spikes were now almost
totally embedded in her body. "Kiss me," he ordered
her.

Half crazy with pain and terror, she nevertheless
tried to comply. He pressed his mouth against hers.
The soft, erotic contact triggered something inside him.
He felt as if his head exploded. His body shook with

sensation and he hugged her against him with all his strength, crushing and stabbing the life out of her as he climaxed. Her body shuddered and bled in his grip.

After she had died, he pulled himself off her and staggered outside. His heart was pounding painfully. He stripped off the body armor and dropped it on the grass. The steel spikes gleamed red, and the metallic hide was stained dark with her blood.

He sat there for a long time, trying to recover his senses. His head was full of pain and death. He had satisfied one of his needs for vengeance—and yet even now, it didn't seem enough. Would he have to kill every living thing, on every planet in the galaxy, before he could rest?

His thoughts were interrupted by a flash of light in the sky. Aton looked up quickly and shaded his eyes. A circular shape was descending toward him, sunlight gleaming on its smooth rim. "Five!" a voice boomed out. "Stay right there, Five. Don't move."

Well, he had known they would come for him eventually. He watched the flier with a dull sense of dread as it circled the cabin. A beam flickered briefly and there was the crack and crackle of wood as trees were severed and bushes burst into flame, clearing an area big enough for the flier to land in. Finally its great silver bulk settled beside the cabin, and a hatch opened.

"Don't touch your weapon, Five. Move and you're dead."

Guards and dorgs poured out of the hatch. Several of the black-uniformed women grabbed him. One examined the Minion man, skewered on the ground. Another checked inside. A third found the bloody spiked armor.

"What is this? You wanted to love her to death?" The guard stared at Aton in puzzlement.

Aton looked up at her blankly. "Love is death," he said.

47.

"If it were my decison, you would be killed," said Oris. She was sitting in the control room of the flier as it skimmed over the Minion landscape. He was lying on the floor at her feet, hog-tied, with a guard standing either side of him. His clothes were ripped and his body ached from the beating they'd administered after dragging him into the vehicle.

"You disobeyed orders, and you burned your dorg," she went on. "That's ample cause for having you publicly sacrificed." She moved a control, and the flier veered suddenly. The display of the terrain below had lit up with white tracers outlining a flight path. A personnel carrier was moving across a field below, firing its beam weapon on docile, bovine creatures scattered across the hillside. They exploded one by one, spattering the hillside with blood, skin, and entrails.

"Unit Seventeen," Oris spoke into a transceiver. "What the hell are you doing? You're supposed to be killing people, not cattle."

There was no reply over the comm link.

She took the flier down. "Come aboard, Seventeen. We're pulling out. Do you understand?"

There was a pause. "Uh, yes, Oris."

She waited while the doors to the cargo bay opened and the carrier rumbled in, joining half a dozen others that she had already picked up. Then she took the flier into the air again, heading back toward its original landing field.

The wraparound video display showed the Minion

210

landscape ravaged by the warriors. Mutilated bodies lay outside homes that had been smashed into kindling. Fires burned wherever a village had stood. The air was hazy with wood smoke.

"As I was saying," Oris went on, "under normal circumstances, you'd be sentenced to a slow death. But the circumstances aren't normal."

She leaned back in her chair and surveyed him with ironic detachment. "The fact is, Five, someone set you up. You were assigned to that area of Minion in the hope that it would trigger you the way it did. It provided the final test of your conditioning: proof that under our care, you've become completely alienated from your former life."

Aton lay on the cold metal floor, his arms and legs throbbing where the ropes cut into his skin. Grimly, he absorbed what she had just said. He realized that his worst suspicions had been correct: all along, someone had been manipulating him. He drew a slow, painful breath. "Tell me who."

She smiled humorlessly, enjoying her position of power over him. She gestured to one of her guards. "Take Five to the storage room, lock him in, and don't release him till we reach orbit."

48.

The last of the fliers rose up from the surface of the planet, heading toward the mother ship waiting above. The mission, such as it was, had been accomplished. It was time to move on.

Aton was dragged out of the cargo bay of Oris's flier, into the mother ship itself. The guards marched him along corridors and into the circular control room. It was just as he remembered it: the starcube, the silver floor, and the white control consoles ranged around the perimeter. Oris and Quentain stood flanked by their dorgs, as they had before. But this time a third figure was present, seated in the pilot's chair.

It took Aton several seconds to recognize the man. "Schenck," he said. It was another name from the past, and it brought another rush of painful memories. Moreover, it seemed impossible. Once again Aton felt as if reality had suddenly twisted around him.

The fat man's lip curled maliciously, and his little dark eyes narrowed to slits. "Yes, Five. It is me, Schenck. Quite correct."

Aton started up onto his feet. "But you were a bounty hunter. I left you on Hvee."

"Show some respect." The guard behind Aton forced him back down onto his knees.

Schenck spread his hands. "I lied to you, Five. I was not a trader, and I was not a bounty hunter either." He turned to Quentain and then to Oris, still with his nasty grin, as if inviting them to share his joke at Aton's expense.

Aton stared at the man. "But you reported Malice—"

"I reported your Minionette to the authorities," Schenck went on. "Oh, yes, that much was true. But it was all worked out with her in advance, Five. I wanted you, but I wanted it to look as if it was your idea to leave your home. So we put you in a position where your behavior would be predictable. Indeed, it was. Your wife let you think it was your idea to leave Hvee, but she took you to Chthon in my ship on my orders."

Aton blinked. He said nothing.

"Betrayed again, Five? Is that what you are thinking?" Schenck eased himself out of his chair and slowly got to his feet. He brushed imaginary dust off his immaculate dark-gray suit and waddled toward Aton. "I decided the Federation might be watching you on Hvee; that is why we wanted you surreptitiously. I did not realize your animal—your pet—might be fitted with surveillance equipment, but we took care of that, didn't we?" He grinned some more.

"Why?" said Aton. The word had a flat, demanding sound.

Schenck's grin slowly faded. "Frankly, Five, I wanted to see you suffer." He was speaking more seriously, more slowly, now. "You had to pay for what you did to the plasma intelligence of Chthon. I work for it, do you see? It knew where to find you. It wanted you back, Five, and I gave it what it wanted. My friends" —he gestured at Oris and Quentain—"just did what I told them to. As they always do. Am I right?" He turned and looked at each of them in turn.

"Yes, sir." They said it in unison. Quentain spoke with a ghost of a smile, as if it didn't cost her anything to humor this fat man. Oris, however, was grim and pale. It obviously didn't sit well with her to admit, in front of Aton, that there was an authority that she had to submit to.

Schenck turned back to Aton. "So you see, I am the one who arranged it all. I ruined your life, Five, and I enjoyed every moment. I have enjoyed telling you about it, and I enjoy the fact that there is nothing you can do about it."

Aton drew a deep breath and let it out slowly. Finally, he understood. Not that it exonerated Oris or Quentain in any way; he craved to hurt them as much as ever. His priorities had changed, that was all.

"So." Schenck put his hands in his pockets. "You look unhappy, Five. Good. You have paid for attempting to murder an intelligence superior to your own."

"Did you kill my father?" He stared straight at the man, trying to see into his mean little eyes.

Schenck gestured vaguely. "There are some things I cannot tell you, because that is not my job. But you will find out soon enough, where you are going. We, you see, are moving on to the next world." He waddled back to his control chair. "The mind of Chthon is inhuman in the purest sense. It despises all forms of organic life, and has assigned us to cause as much pain and death as possible." He sank into the chair. "But your part in this is over. You will make your own little trip. Do you remember a man named Bedeker?"

The name jolted Aton. It was from his more distant past. He remembered the gene labs of Luna, and the zoo of human freaks that Bedeker had maintained. "A geneticist," he said. "He was some kind of extension of Chthon."

"Is," Schenck corrected him. "Bedeker is alive and well, Five, as is the mind of Chthon. You will pay him a visit." He turned to Oris. "Has the navigation computer in my cargo transport vehicle been reset?"

"Yes, sir." She still avoided his eyes, as if pride inhibited her from directly acknowledging his authority.

"Good. Take Five to the ship, activate its program, lock him in it, and eject it." Schenck turned back to Aton. "It will be a two-day trip, Five. When you arrive, I assure you, it will seem quite worthwhile."

The guard behind Aton grabbed him under his arms

and hauled him onto his feet. Abruptly, Aton realized that he was about to be separated, maybe permanently, from Schenck, Oris, Quentain, and all the others.

"No," he said. He braced himself, wrenched free, turned, and grabbed the guard's sword. To be deprived of revenge would be intolerable. He hurled the sword like a spear, aiming for Schenck's fat belly.

One of the dorgs leaped forward with inhuman speed and knocked the sword out of the air with its front paw. The weapon clattered harmlessly to the deck.

Aton was already running forward, heading for Oris, his hands outstretched, his face contorted with rage. She stepped back, looking disconcerted. But another of the dorgs jumped into his path. It reared up with its teeth bared, its paws ready to grip him in a deadly embrace.

He stopped. He glanced toward Quentain, but she, too, was protected by a dorg. Aton clenched his fists and cursed them, overwhelmed with impotent rage. Guards rushed up and seized him. He submitted, still glaring at the three people he most craved to hurt and kill.

The dorgs padded back to their original positions. Oris looked at Aton as if she wanted to order his immediate execution, but she said nothing.

Schenck shook his head. "Five, it has been very entertaining, playing with you for the past few months. But you are now beginning to irritate me." He gestured to the guards. "Kindly take him out of here."

49.

Schenck's cargo transport was the same one in which Aton and Malice had fled from Hvee. The guards shut him in it, but left him free to roam the empty corridors and shaftways. He floated through them, alone in the ship, until he found the tiny cabin where he had huddled with the emp, during the days when he had been waiting and wondering what was going to happen to him. The restraint webbing was still hooked across the bunk where he had left it, and a pile of emergency-rations wrappers lay on the floor.

Aton went to the central shaft and kicked up it to the control room. There was the G-couch where she had sat. Here were the controls. He steadied himself against the panel as the ship's attitude thrusters fired and the small rocket engines nudged it out of the mother ship's cargo bay and into space.

A pause, then another lurch and a distant roaring of the motors. He moved to the couch, rested on it, and watched the screens. On one side they showed the face of the planet Minion against the blackness of space. On the other side was the bulk of the mother ship, the doors of its cargo bay slowly closing after ejecting the little transport vehicle into the void.

For a long moment, nothing happened; then the mother ship started moving slowly away. Its drive increased power and it diminished more and more rapidly, till it was a pinpoint among the stars.

Aton was left still orbiting Minion. Soon, he guessed, Federation forces would come to investigate the sudden loss of contact with the transmitter that had been in the king's palace. By then, Schenck, Oris, Quentain, and their warriors would be raining death on some other world at the other end of the galaxy. He imagined them encountering some unexpected resistance, imagined their ship's defenses overwhelmed, so that it fell helplessly and burned up in a planet's atmosphere, roasting everyone inside it. He saw Oris's face turning black as the heat consumed her, Quentain's flesh bubbling and popping like meat in an oven.

He shook his head angrily. The fantasies were futile; he had failed, and he should admit it.

Over at the control panel, the navigation computer clicked, following its preset program, and the vehicle's own drive came to life. Aton watched passively. He had already checked the controls. They were completely dead; there was no way to override them manually. The ship was going to take him to preset coordinates, and until he got there, there was nothing he could do.

G-forces pressed him gently into his seat. The face of Minion began to shift and recede. Schenck's little cargo transport departed smoothly, heading into the void.

50.

Something was blotting out the stars. As Aton watched the viewscreen he saw a black shape at the center slowly expanding, obscuring the white pinpoints around it.

The ship was barely moving now. After two days it had decelerated and emerged into normal spacetime near a small planetary system—exactly which one he had no way of knowing. The sun at the center was large and yellow. There were several planets, but none of them was close enough to check visually.

The ship had drifted slowly for an hour or more, its reaction motors firing intermittently in accordance with the preset program. Now it seemed to be approaching something like a black stormcloud floating in the void.

Aton checked the proximity detector. Whatever the object was, it had mass. It showed on the radar as being disk-shaped, a few hundred feet in diameter, rotating slowly. Its edges rippled and curled. The ship drifted toward it like a fly into a spiderweb, closer, and still closer.

A slithering, rasping sound resonated through the hull, as if the entire vehicle were being wrapped in something firm but sticky. All the screens went completely black, and all external sensors went dead. The shell of the ship creaked and groaned as the black stuff pressed around it. The floor lurched under Aton's feet and then was still.

He floated alone in the control room, looking from one blank screen to the next. The navigation computer

chimed softly, signifying that its program had ended
and it was returning to manual mode. Evidently the
vehicle had brought Aton to his intended destination.
Theoretically, now, he could reprogram it and head
someplace new. But if he did that, he'd be taking the
stuff outside with him, and he would be flying blind.

There was a muffled tapping sound above his head.
He looked up quickly, not knowing what to expect.
There was an emergency airlock in the nose of the
ship, directly above the control room. Something was
trying to get in.

Aton scanned the controls. He found the emergency
override to seal the ship against any entry, reached
toward it, but didn't touch it. Whatever it was out
there had been instrumental in everything that had
happened to him. He had to know what it was. He
could not evade a confrontation.

A motor whined, and the outer airlock door opened.
Aton turned his back to the control panel and waited,
staring upward. Something thumped into the airlock,
but there was no window in the inner door, so he had
no way of seeing what was there.

The outer door closed, and air hissed into the compartment. Aton had already searched the ship for weapons; there was nothing on the ship that would enable
him to defend himself. A plastic tray lay close by, with
the remnants of his lunch still on it. He vaguely imagined using that as a shield, but the idea was laughable:
any projectile would penetrate it, and a heat gun would
melt it instantly.

The inner door slid slowly open, and a figure drifted
in. It was a man: tall, gaunt, bearded, with deep-set
haunted eyes. He moved down into the control room,
steadying himself clumsily against the wall. He reached
the acceleration couch opposite Aton and rested there,
turning his bearded face toward him.

"Bedeker," Aton said.

The man gave an awkward, twisted smile. "Didn't
they tell you to expect me?" His speech was slurred

and accented in a way that was similar to Schenck's.
He gestured vaguely, as if he had trouble maintaining
coordination.

"You're dead," said Aton. "I saw you die. On
Luna."

Bedeker looked around the control room. His eyes
moved quickly, but he seemed to have trouble focusing, and he took in the details as if he had never been
in a ship before. "Bedeker's *intelligence* never died,"
he said. "As for the body—this one is a simulation.
It's made of SOMA. The black stuff outside is SOMA,
too. That's the name I've given it, anyway. Sentient
Organic Multicellular Automaton."

Aton watched him warily, keeping as much distance
as possible between them. "SOMA is something to do
with Chthon?"

Bedeker nodded. He opened and closed his mouth
as if exercising the jaw muscles. He raised one hand
and touched his own face, feeling the shape of it. He
moved like a poorly programmed robot, still testing its
coordination. "'We are currently near Chthon's orbit," he went on, "though the planet is on the other
side of the sun at present. You'll remember that when
you destroyed the plasma intelligence at the center of
Chthon, it was blown into space. Some of it coalesced
here. The structure of the plasma could not be recovered, but the program for its intelligence was stored
on a molecular level, just as a single sperm cell and a
single ovum contain a program to build an entire human being. You see, that was our contingency plan, so
that Chthon and myself could survive."

"*Our* plan?"

"We—I—am a vast group of cells. Clever cells,
Five. So clever, we can even imitate a human being.
You see?" He spread out his arms and looked down at
himself. "Even these clothes that I'm wearing are
SOMA cells. They've been reprogrammed to behave
that way, temporarily. But they can change." As he
spoke, his jacket seemed to become plastic. It passed

quickly through a spectrum of colors. It billowed around him, then relaxed.

"Malice," Aton said softly, remembering her transformation into a black, puttylike substance that had shifted and flowed.

"Yes." Bedeker smiled. His eyes glittered. "She became SOMA. I started the process in her almost a year ago, on Luna."

"You infected her while she was in your gene labs?"

Bedeker nodded. "SOMA cells can replace human cells gradually, one by one, precisely imitating their function. Even nerve cells in the brain. The victim doesn't know it's happening. Until, later, the SOMA cells are activated. Then they become sentient and acquire their own group consciousness. They may choose to continue behaving like a human being—or they may choose not to." He gave Aton a serene smile, like a zealot who had just described nirvana.

"So Schenck is a SOMA entity, too."

"Of course. Some of SOMA fell back to the surface of Chthon. We maintain a form of mental communication. We established the camp on the surface of Chthon with the aid of Oris and Quentain. They aren't part of us; they're humans, sociopaths who just happened to suit our purposes. The warriors, likewise. The other guards, though, and the dorgs—those are all SOMA."

"So Schenck came to Hvee," Aton said, piecing things together. "He found me. He activated the cells that had taken over Malice—"

"Not quite. Your father was also a SOMA entity; Malice inadvertently infected him when you both arrived on Hvee. She and he remained dormant, unaware of what had happened to them, till Schenck arrived. He activated the cells in Aurelius, who did the same for Malice. All it takes is close contact, or exchange of bodily fluids, for the information to pass from cell to cell. In minutes, the SOMA organism acquires cellular consciousness. There's a crucial moment of transition, though, in which the cells are switching from dormant to active role. The whole system can break down—in which case everything dies."

"Which is what happened to Aurelius?"

Bedeker nodded. "Fortunately, he had passed the programming to Malice just beforehand. And in her case, it was entirely successful. Oh, there was some deterioration in her physical appearance. Once the cells acquire their active SOMA identity, they find it hard to sustain a simulation of a human being. That was why we made all the dorgs and all the women guards look the same; we perfected the design and shared the work of sustaining it. This Bedeker replica, which we created so we could communicate with you and convince you of the truth, is an extra drain on our resources."

Aton took a slow, deep breath. "All right." He nodded. "You've succeeded. I believe you. It explains everything that's happened. But you didn't bring me out here just for a conversation."

Once again Bedeker contrived the awkward, twisted smile. He let go of the couch and started drifting very slowly toward Aton. "We brought you here, Five, to conduct a delicate operation under the most carefully controlled circumstances, at the heart of SOMA."

"An operation?" Aton edged backward.

"No, no, not what you think. We've finished taking revenge on you, Five. It's time for you to join us now."

"What do you mean?" He eyed the shaftway leading out of the control room. Bedeker was blocking his access to it. He wondered if he could kick up and over the man. Bedeker's SOMA body still seemed sluggish and uncoordinated. But even if Aton could evade him—what then?

Bedeker laughed. "It's much too late to escape, Five. Malice infected you months ago. Not her fault; she didn't know. As I said, intimate contact will communicate it. So, right now, you're already one hundred percent SOMA. Dormant, of course—but not for much longer." He pushed himself closer. "One touch is all it will take." He held up the forefinger of his right hand. As Aton watched, the fingernail extended itself, growing into a curved blade. "One little scratch." He grinned, exposing irregular, budlike teeth, and a mouth that seemed incompletely formed, lacking a tongue. "You'll like it, Five. It's a superior form of existence. Human beings are like unintelligent pests by comparison. That's why we're exterminating them."

Beside Aton's hand was the fire button controlling the reaction motors of the ship, used for maneuvering in free fall. He flipped its safety cover up and jammed his thumb on it. Hypergolic fuel flowed into combustion chambers. Flame erupted from the engines at the tail. It seared the layer of SOMA enveloping the ship.

The vehicle lurched. Aton was prepared for it. Bedeker fell backward, flailing his arms, and his face seemed to melt. He shouted in pain. SOMA was one group entity; Bedeker's cells were sharing the experience of the cells being fried alive by rocket exhaust.

Aton seized the plastic food tray beside him, held it on the palm of his hand, and swung it into Bedeker's chest, knocking him up toward the emergency hatch. Bedeker somersaulted backward. His body was shrinking into a lumpy black thing, merging with the pseudo-clothes around it. A strange, high-pitched keening noise emitted from the cavity where his mouth had been. He bounced off the edge of the escape hatch and fell into the airlock.

Aton activated the inner door. Bedeker reached out a boneless arm that writhed like a pseudopod, but he was too late. The door slid shut.

Aton turned back to the control panel. He hit the keys to fire all of the attitude thrusters. Small motors along the length of the ship came to life, searing the SOMA entity with pinpricks of flame. The ship started spinning. Aton touched the controls again, increased the rate of rotation. Centrifugal force threw him hard against the wall—and threw the layer of SOMA off

the outside of the ship. In the viewscreens, the stars
reappeared.

Aton reversed the attitude thrusters, canceling the
spin. He increased the thrust of the reaction motors to
maximum, blasting out of SOMA's embrace. Then he
turned on the grav-drive. In the rear viewscreens,
black strands and blobs fell away behind the ship like
a ripped spiderweb.

Aton turned to the navigation computer. If he could
remember some planetary coordinates, he could reprogram it. Otherwise, he would have to plunge blindly
into space, where the odds against emerging near a
star system would be billions to one.

But there was one set of coordinates that anyone
knew who'd ever spent time on interstellar transport,
as he had. The coordinates for Old Earth.

He punched them into the keyboard, then fell back
onto the couch as the ship turned toward its new
destination.

51.

During the first few hours of the trip, he scoured the control room. Wearing a biohazard suit that he found in the utility cargo bay, he vacuumed every particle of dirt and wiped every surface with cleaning fluid. He found a black, gummy SOMA residue where Bedeker had scraped against the edge of the emergency hatch. It flowed sluggishly toward his glove when he reached out to touch it. Cleaning fluid didn't seem to have any effect on it, so he went to the supply room and found bottles of battery acid. When he prepared a strong solution of the acid and wiped it across the black goo, it writhed and rippled as it slowly dissolved. In his imagination, he heard it screaming.

If Bedeker had been telling the truth, the black stuff was not so different from Aton himself. His cells were now SOMA cells, dumbly imitating the human cells they had replaced. It would only take one tiny particle of Bedeker's SOMA residue to contaminate Aton's cells and reprogram them, triggering his transformation to cellular consciousness and the final, irrevocable loss of his human identity.

In some ways, the concept didn't seem particularly threatening. He already felt totally alienated from his fellow humans. It would not trouble him greatly if humanity, as a species, was exterminated. He might even have surrendered willingly to Bedeker, except for one thing: he had committed himself to vengeance. If SOMA was the entity that had robbed him of his home, his father, and his wife, then somehow SOMA must be punished.

He found extra air tanks for his biohazard suit in the cargo bay. He had to switch tanks every six hours. Whenever he did so, he scoured the threads on the connector carefully with dilute acid before screwing it into place. Twice he found a suspicious filmy black residue on the outside of the air hose, trying to penetrate the seal.

He ate and drank sparingly, at wide intervals. He donned disposable gloves before opening the food packs, and wiped his faceplate with the acid solution before opening it. He used a white cloth, and found a faint black residue on it every time.

When he slept, he dreamed of blackness closing around him, spreading over the suit, somehow filtering through it, touching his skin, entering his blood, turning him into some new life form—a dorg, or one of the sexless female guards on Chthon. Each time, he woke with a start, gasping for breath, his whole body trembling.

The trip to Earth took four days. By the end of that time he was choking on his own odor but no longer dared to open the faceplate. He spent all his waking hours cleaning and recleaning the control room and the outside of the suit, mumbling dementedly about dirt, cells, and vengeance. He was no longer entirely sane; but he was still a human being—superficially, at least.

52.

The people of Luna picked up his mumbled radio messages warning of a cellular life form that had infected him and was spreading through the galaxy. They told him to identify himself. As soon as they realized who he was, they sent robot drones to intercept his ship, and expert systems to comunicate with him.

They coaxed him out of the control room, into space. His biohazard suit swelled like a balloon; it had never been intended for use in a vacuum. Still, it sustained him while spidery metal arms transferred him to a sealed, sterile environment. High-energy beams then incinerated his ship and any form of life that might still be clinging to it. He was sedated, and they took him to the gene labs on Luna itself.

Time became fragmented. Life became a series of intermittent waking moments, trapped in a white chamber, communicating with faces on screens. One of the faces he recognized: a petite, sharp-featured woman with alert eyes and intelligent features. Samantha Smith, the systems analyst; he had dealt with her before, before he had been robbed of his life—

"Tell me everything that happened to you, Aton."

Everything. A robot hand administered another shot of sedative. He was floating. Past and present time merged together. Everything; the word resonated.

"I'm no longer human. If you do an analysis—"

"We know. The analysis shows an entirely alien, allotropic cell with silent genes. We're studying it. Now tell me everything that happened to you."

"I was born on Hvee—"

"Start with the camp on Chthon. Tell me why you murdered Alix." The voice was gentle, but the face on the screen looked grimly serious.

He thought of Alix and her kind, warm touch. The lovemaking in her room. His anger rose up. "She betrayed me. She had to be punished."

"No. She cared for you. She risked her life for you."

He twisted in the soft padded bed that held him like a cocoon. "They must all be punished!"

"Aton. Listen to me. You're not making any sense. Tell me everything. Were you in the war party that massacred the people of Minion? Why did you kill those people?"

He saw a red-haired woman, lover and mother, cruel beauty, a look of amused disdain, rejecting him. "I killed Malice."

"That's impossible. She disappeared after she left you on Chthon. We believe she was contaminated with the same cell system that has infected you. But we don't know. You have to help us, Aton. If you help us, we will help you."

That focused his attention. "You'll help me destroy SOMA?"

"Of course."

He didn't trust her. She too would betray him. But he could use her assistance until she turned against him; and then he could kill her too.

"It began on Hvee, the day my father died. . . ."

53.

He talked to Samantha Smith for many hours. She listened, always attentive, with eyes that seemed to understand him even through the medium of the videoscreen. Her neutrality, her quiet voice, and her patience were strangely seductive, and he found himself entering a detached state of mind in which his life seemed to lie like a landscape far below, with features that he could point out for her interest.

He became a tour guide to his own timeline. As he looked back at his own actions, he was faintly surprised by his ruthlessness. Still he felt no remorse; it was right that people around him should have paid for the crimes that had been committed against him.

"But SOMA was your real enemy, Aton," Samantha reminded him once in a while. "You know that."

He didn't argue; he knew that this was so.

They cut back some of the psychoactive medication. Aton found his thoughts coming into clearer focus. The events he had described to her, which previously seemed so distant, now haunted him in close-up. She made him describe them again, and for the first time, he hesitated over the most brutal details.

"Would you kill me the way you killed other innocent people?" she asked at one point.

"Only if you betray me."

"But they didn't betray you. You see that now. SOMA manipulated you, and manipulated them. No one betrayed you."

She was talking more to him, and listening less. Her

voice was insistent; it seemed to come from inside his head. Strangely, he did not resent its intrusion. It made him feel less isolated, more human. He still told himself that he couldn't trust her to any degree; but without realizing it, he was starting to depend on her gentle commentary.

"SOMA was my enemy," he repeated. "Yes. I know."

"The people you killed did not betray you. They were innocent people. Some of them even tried to help you."

He blinked. The room containing him suddenly seemed much more tangible and real than it had before. He looked at all the equipment arrayed around him, and the big videoscreen standing opposite. How long had he been in here?

"They were not your enemies," she repeated insistently.

"But I killed them?" It no longer seemed to make sense.

"You committed atrocities. You inflicted terrible suffering and death." Abruptly, she cut the link. The screen went blank.

He was left alone inside his own head, confronted by the enormity of what he had done. "Come back!" he shouted.

She returned to him an hour later. By that time, he was huddled in a ball, rocking to and fro, crying and clutching himself. "SOMA took away everything. It killed my father. It killed Malice. It killed my pet. It hurt me. It disfigured me."

"That explains why you did what you did," she said calmly. "But the fact remains: the people you killed were innocent."

"Then I should be punished. But I already have been punished. I have nothing."

"There's no need for any further punishment. You were insane. You were not responsible for your own actions."

He stared at her image, wanting to believe what she had just said.

"You can still atone for your crimes," she went on. "That is the proper answer."

"How? By killing SOMA?"

She shook her head. "There has been enough killing."

"But it destroyed me. If we don't destroy it, it will destroy everyone."

"Aton, when you are facing an enemy, you don't necessarily have to destroy him in order to be secure. There is another way."

"What?" he stared blankly at her image on the screen.

She shrugged. "You can persuade him to be your friend."

"But SOMA despises human life. It looks on us as vermin."

Samantha shrugged. She smiled. "Then we must induce SOMA to change its mind."

54.

They put him in a ship and sent him back into space. The ship was a crude and simple shell built around a grav-drive and a navigation computer, nothing more. There was only one cabin, and its interior was bare, containing no furnishings or amenities of any kind. It was open to the vacuum of space and heated to a temperature slightly above freezing. Aton was happy enough in these primitive conditions: he no longer had need for comfort, oxygen, or warmth.

His only luxury was a small mirror. He derived a peculiar satisfaction from seeing his own face remade, free from all the blemishes that had been inflicted during his initiation in the camp on Chthon. He looked human again—which was ironic, since he was far less human now than he had been before. In fact, he was now capable of rearranging his features in any human or inhuman form he chose.

The little ship took him to the planetary system that had been programmed into its computer. Aton was not bored during the four-day journey; he spent the time listening to the new music of his cells, exploring the sentience inside himself.

The ship emerged in normal spacetime and spent several hours scanning for a small, special object that was known to be floating somewhere in this region. Having successfully found it and locked on, it spent another day moving into position for rendezvous.

Finally, the ship announced to him that its task was complete. Aton roused himself from his inner contem-

plation. He looked out and saw SOMA as he had seen
it before: a black shape obscuring the stars. It was no
longer shredded and torn; it had coalesced again into a
disk, turning slowly, warming itself from the distant
sun that also shone on Chthon.

Its presence resonated now with his constituent cells.
It called to him as a piece of itself. He stood up, naked
as he had been throughout the journey. He opened
the ship's hatch and stepped into space. He needed no
pressure suit; the vacuum could no longer hurt him,
and nor could the temperature of space, provided he
moved so that the sun warmed each side of his body in
turn.

The ship had stopped less than a hundred feet from
the SOMA disk. Aton kicked himself toward the black
cellular mass floating in front of him. It rippled expectantly, anticipating his union with it.

He impacted gently in its center. Its surface was soft
and sticky, and it surged up around him, holding him
possessively, claiming him as its own.

He scratched a tiny incision in the sticky black surface beside him, touched it with his moistened finger,
and waited.

At first there was no perceptible change. Then he
felt a faint trembling in the membrane that held him.
The trembling became a vibration, and ripples spread
outward as if the disk were the surface of a pond into
which a stone had been thrown. Suddenly it convulsed,
twisting under him in a spasm that almost seemed to
rend it apart. He clung to it, afraid of being ejected
into space. The stars turned around him. Gradually,
then, the spasms subsided, and it relaxed.

We are one, now, he thought. The thought reflected
back at him from the billions of cells that shared it.
The thought was a chorus of values and intent.

Aton carefully visualized the boundaries of his physical body and started struggling to disengage himself
from the sticky black stuff. Already, he found, some
of him had merged with it, and some of it had merged

with him, so that it was hard to tell where the separation should occur. Well, if he left some of himself here, and took some of it with him, it would make no difference.

He finally freed himself and kicked back toward the open hatch of the ship. He had accomplished the first stage in his mission, but there was much more still to do.

He was, of course, no longer human in any sense. He had surrendered his human identity back on Luna as the price he had to pay for his own redemption. Still, his cells could remember his past as a human being. He remembered, for instance, his last conversation with Samantha Smith.

He had still been in the sterile tank, communicating with her over the video link, but his period of confinement was almost over.

"We have completed our molecular analysis of the tissue sample we took from you," she told him. "We now understand SOMA—or rather, our computers do. Only a machine intelligence can decode something so complex."

"What's your plan?" He asked the question fatalistically, suspecting that whatever she said, it would offer no hope of restoring to him his life as a normal person.

"We're going to activate your dormant SOMA cells," she told him. "You will make the transition from a human replica to a pure cellular automaton. But the program we'll give them will be different from other SOMA entities. We've made changes in the code."

She went on to explain that they had engineered a new set of imperatives. His SOMA cells would not seek to eradicate human life; instead, their new program would impel them to protect it. They would no longer be driven to reproduce themselves and infect other organisms as a way of disseminating themselves like a virus throughout the galaxy. Instead, SOMA cells would feel a need to unite with larger and larger aggregates of their own kind, returning ultimately to their birthplace on Chthon.

The new program was designed to replicate itself indefinitely. He was the source, the primary vector; each SOMA form that he touched would be reprogrammed in his image. Thus, SOMA would not be destroyed—it had already spread so widely there was no easy way to eradicate it. Instead, it would be subverted from within. It would be reprogrammed to become benign instead of malignant.

Aton drifted in through the ship's hatch, turned, and closed it behind him. The ship had monitored his contact with the SOMA disk, and its systems had already transmitted a report back to Luna. Everything, so far, had worked as planned.

Aton waited while the ship turned, searching for the planet Chthon. It was currently occupying a position in its orbit on the far side of the bright yellow star that was its sun.

On Chthon, there would be more SOMA life forms to receive the message that Aton carried in his cells. From there, he would travel perhaps to Xerva, the metal world, where some of Schenck's SOMA servants probably still remained, overseeing weapons production in the automated factories.

Ultimately, Aton would find Schenck and his war party. He would merge not only with Schenck and his dorgs and guards, but with Oris, Quentain, and their warriors as well. This would be the one exception to his imperative against infecting any additional human hosts with the SOMA form. It would also be his ultimate victory: not to punish his onetime oppressors, but to force them to become replicas of himself.

Eventually, he might encounter the SOMA aggregate that had once configured itself as Malice. No SOMA cell group could really be separate from any other part, for they all shared a common identity. But he imagined that there might be some strange, special pleasure in merging his cells with hers.

The ship accelerated on a parabola toward Chthon. The planet came into view as a tiny green pinpoint against the darkness of space, and Aton considered how it would feel when the SOMA entities obeyed their new imperative to return and reassemble there. He would become part of an immense group consciousness, alien to humanity yet symbiotic with it. He would even achieve a form of immortality, since there seemed no aging process built into the SOMA form.

He now felt no regret at the transformation that had been forced on him. Already, as a SOMA entity, he had achieved something he had never really known before: a sense of unity. As a person, he had always been haunted by the stigma of being a half-breed, and had felt alienated from others. Now his cells were a chorus of separate yet meshing identities, united as a group, and promising powers as yet untested.

Alone in the airless metal cabin, heading down toward the surface of Chthon, he felt a strange kind of satisfaction. He had fulfilled none of the obsessions that had ruled his life. And yet, he was at peace with himself, and content.

Afterword

The SOMA entity in this novel is not entirely fictitious. In the last ten years, mathematicians have become interested in "cellular automata": cells patterns that follow very simple additive growth rules, but evolve in complicated ways that seem to imitate life itself. There is no theoretical reason why such an entity could not display intelligence.

The availability of microcomputers has made it possible for many of us to experiment with cellular automata at home. These forms of pseudo-life appear as patterns on the screen that grow from an initial seed to form structures that can be vast, complex, and very beautiful.

Programs to generate two families of cellular automata (the two-dimensional type and the newer linear type) are now available for IBM-PC with graphics adapter, PCjr, or true IBM-compatibles. For additional information, send a self-addressed stamped business-size envelope to:

> Cell Systems
> 594 Broadway, Room 1208
> New York, NY 10012

(IBM, IBM-PC, and PCjr are registered trademarks of International Business Machines Corporation.)

About The Author

Charles Platt's science fiction includes *Twilight of the City*, a study of urban decay at the turn of the century, and *Free Zone,* which applies a humorous treatment to traditional SF themes. His nonfiction includes computer books and the highly praised *Dream Makers* series, profiling fifty-seven of the best known authors in the science fiction field.

Platt is the onetime editor of *New Worlds*, a radical British magazine of the late 1960s. He now lives in New York City, where in addition to writing novels, he is science fiction editor for the publisher Franklin Watts.

In the vast intergalactic world of the future
the soldiers battle

NOT FOR GLORY

JOEL ROSENBERG

author of the bestselling
Guardian of the Flame series

Only once in the history of the Metzadan merce-
nary corps has a man been branded traitor. That
man is Bar-El, the most cunning military mind in
the universe. Now his nephew, Inspector-General
Hanavi, must turn to him for help. What begins as
one final mission is transformed into a series of
campaigns that takes the Metzadans from world to
world, into intrigues, dangers, and treacherous dip-
lomatic games, where a strategist's highly irregular maneuvers and a master assassin's swift blade
may prove the salvation of the planet—or its ultimate ruin . . .